XENTU SECRET

Lost Xentu
~ Book 4 ~

MARIE JUDSON

INDIES UNITED PUBLISHING HOUSE, LLC
P.O. BOX 3071
QUINCY, IL 62305-3071

OTHER BOOKS by MARIE JUDSON

CHAPTER

1

Yanda held her son Zami and daughter Seiti tight as she took in the elven forest around them. They'd done it. Against all odds, they'd gotten Seiti off Blaz, the most heavily barricaded and hostile of all planets in the Known Universe.

And now the Blaz knew. They'd discovered their prize child-weapon missing. And were searching for her. So they'd jumped across lightyears to get to the dome of the Neya elves.

Ilan stood next to Yanda, tall, red-haired techie Qontaqian who used AI and magic interchangeably. Never having been to Terlond, much less the planet's hidden forest of the elves, he stared into tall trees where rope ladders and slatted ramps connected glimpses of treehouses high above. "So we're not really seeing sky? There's a dome over the whole elven forest?"

"The dome's transparent," Yanda said. "You'll see sky once we get out from under the trees. Maybe we should get to the bunker." She turned her question to Merne who stood apart from their small group. "Do you think?"

Merne, lion-eyed elf-woman, tall, sturdy, brown-green braids looped up from leaf-shaped ears, stood apart from their little group. Having transported them across lightyears in an instant, she barely looked winded. She stepped closer. "I have to get back to the Sarsefi. Yeah, bunker's probably the best place for you, though you should be safe anywhere under the dome."

She touched Seiti's cheek, with that mix on her face that they all seemed to carry, of admiration and fear. Could the young girl really be trusted? She'd been in Tiklet, a sophisticated training facility so secret Yanda and the others had only recently learned of it, undetectable on Blaz, a planet so heavily mined and toxic its only atmosphere was under domes that pocked its surface like a disease.

"We'll be back with the Sarsefi in no time," Merne said, moving away into the woods and then she was gone.

Yanda said, "This way," and started leading them in the direction of the bunker—long subterranean refuge used by the elves in times of trouble. It had at least three levels underground, that Yanda knew about.

Seiti, holding her hand, glanced over at her half-elf half-brother. She was fascinated by him, clearly. If she felt anger toward a brother who'd appeared into her mother's life while she was held captive in another star-system, she showed no signs of it. "So this is where you're from? You grew up in treehouses?"

Zami glanced up at his mother, eyes swirling inside the irises. There was a question in his mind sent only to her.

"Zami and I only lived here a month or so after we escaped from the Citadel, in the City." Yanda indicated a direction, looking back, but only trees were visible. "So we've both only lived in treehouses the same amount of time."

"Can we stay in one? You have to climb rope ladders? How do you get up to them?"

"You can make them come to you. Or just jump." Zami rose into the air, grabbing a rope thirty feet up.

"Wow!" Seiti clapped, grinning.

Ilan had seen him "fly" on the ship so he wasn't astonished though his eyes twinkled with admiration.

The tree lined path opened out to only low bushes and sky emerged above, an odd pumpkin-orange color from the Terlondian sun. At least it was not the smoldering, dark orange of Dondar, where Yanda and the fems had been held captive for a year and a half, and breathed gratefully in the scent of flowering vines that climbed over the nearly obscured bunker.

Seiti gazed toward the slate color of the refuge's curved roof and her red-black hair crackled with energy.

"You sense something?" Ilan asked, studying the slender young girl he'd helped to free.

Then he glanced at Yanda. "Do you really think it's safer here than on Elznap?" he asked her.

Yanda gestured toward a peak. "Vashal. That's where the Neyna circle sits in a crystal pyramid and keeps the protective dome in place. Nothing can be detected through it."

"I can tell there's a lot going on down here." Seiti hurried toward the steps leading into the first level underground.

"I'm not sure we'll sleep in the same treehouse," Yanda said.

From close behind them, she heard voices. Elves approached from the edge of the forest, Zamani at the lead.

He strode quickly to Zami and scooped him into his arms, resting his forehead to his son's for a long moment.

Yanda knew thoughts ran between them that she could not detect but he included her in a loving greeting, placing a hand on Seiti's head. "Welcome." His voice shook slightly as he looked down into her clever face and eyes that queried deeply.

Then he turned to Ilan and reached out a hand. "Welcome to Rotoul." He bowed his head toward their clasped hands.

Ilan returned the gesture, eyes slightly narrowed. "I thank you. It's an enchanting place."

"Isn't it though?" Zamani moved finally to Yanda. Bending, with Zami on his hip, he placed a kiss on her check.

He wants to win me back, she thought. But only to keep Zami here. And now he's trying to coax Seiti into admiration, of the place, of him. It was an unworthy thought. He'd never been anything but courteous with her. She didn't like the suspicious attitude her thoughts took but couldn't avoid them.

Then gentle humming forest world vibrations enfolded her like an embrace. Loving sensations seemed to emanate from the plants. The sea, in the distance, charged with the magical energies of its sentient sea creatures, where she'd lived for a time with the sea elves, sent a siren cry, calling her.

Finally, much closer, just beyond the bunker, the Great Stone, Shalt, pulsed ambient caresses through her heart. The message—fond but demanding—said, *you are of us.*

"Thank you. I'm happy to be back close to you." Where did that comment come from? She was far from happy. Yet her soul seemed to speak in place of her mind and she knew, yes, she loved the Great Stone, and this amazing land, even the elves. She just couldn't help suspicion that they would somehow take Zami from her.

She shook these thoughts away, coming to her senses as Zami reached out and wound his fingers in her hair. "Right, Mommy?"

"Sorry, Button. Could you say it again?" Yanda gave her son her full attention.

"We don't mind a smaller treehouse. Didn't you hear Daddy?" Glowing in the circle of Zamani's arm, Zami's gaze was even with hers as he crinkled a scolding grin-frown at her.

Ilan, at her side, seemed to bridle. Yanda knew he felt protective of both her kids. He'd been with Zami for months on the ship, the Sarsefi, and had invested a great deal in helping to save her daughter. Now this handsome, commanding elf, as tall as him but with a presence that defied description, walked into their lives. Next to him, three others, sharing his height, velvet skin of varying shades from plum to indigo, casually emanated power, in clothes of tailored fit, fibers seeming to have been peeled from the trees and plants, in greens, dark brown hues, with bright gold and burgundy highlights.

Between her own tumbling thoughts and Ilan's clear discomfort, Yanda managed to focus. "Absolutely. The smallest treehouse will be living in heaven."

"I want to see." But Seiti was already starting down the stairs to the bunker just as they all heard the mind-call that seemed to come from the air itself.

"The Lark and Sarsefi are under attack." Shalt's voice in Yanda's head was electric with waves of urgency.

"Aren't they cloaked?" she asked, following her daughter into the bunker. "Come on, second level."

"Yanda, help us." A cry for aid from the powerful elder, Shouma, who'd trained her in all her mind skills during their captivity, sent terror into Yanda's bones. Shouma never asked for help. Other messages collided in her mind. She stumbled, trying to stand.

"Was that Shouma? They're in trouble." Ilan raced to Yanda, bracing her.

A gangly young elf strode in, clothes jangling with bits of space detritus, sewn-on shards of metal, plaz, and melted, hardened glass of sapphire and coral. "I'll stay with the kids."

"Arsat, right?" Yanda said. "Where are we supposed to be going?"

The elf teen grinned and moved toward Zami and Seiti. "You can go on to Vashal."

"Oh. Okay," Yanda mumbled to the retreating back.

Ilan gripped the bag that never left his shoulder. It contained his Mons—advanced Qontaqian computer. He adjusted the wide strap, prepared to accompany her anywhere.

Zamani hit the bottom step in a run. "Quickly." He gestured to come.

"Shalt's cave or Vashal?" Yanda asked, a rumbling conversation in her head from the Stone vying for attention.

Shalt lost the immediate battle as Zamani led the way outside. Yanda kissed her children's heads.

Seiti said to into her mind, "I should come with you."

Yanda gripped her daughter's shoulders. "Soon. Let me see what they want."

Soon they were soaring toward Vashal's sharp peak. Gusts of wind snagged them as they swept upward. Yanda caught the scent of wild herbs that grew on the mountainside as they swept close, Zamani keeping arms around Yanda and Ilan, guiding them through the air without visible effort.

Yanda glanced back at forest stretching to sea as they landed lightly on a deck flanked by tall windows. One slid open and they entered a hall that ran along the side of the crystal pyramid, its wall slanted and translucent. Low lighting lit only their feet on soft carpet.

Zamani pressed his hand next to a thick stone door. A panel slid away revealing an antechamber. They crossed to tall narrow door slanting inward.

They stepped into the breathtaking peak of the pyramid. A dozen high stone seats circled inside the three glowing walls that met above in a sharp point, the peak's apex.

The magnificent seats, each reached by steps and carved from the mountain, surrounded a black pool.

An aged elf, with weathered skin and silvering hair, sat on each of the stone seats. One of them beckoned to Yanda.

CHAPTER

2

Ilan held back, standing in the doorway, unsure where to be.

"Please." Zamani gestured to seats along the wall, also carved from the mountain.

Ilan sat as requested. He itched to pull out his Mons. Instead, he set his bag aside and folded his hands, studying the noble-looking elves in their tall seats, facing each other around the strange dark pool. Though still, the waters seemed to pulse energy.

He watched Yanda climb to the seat vacated by the elder elf and settle, without fear, as if she'd done this before. She closed her eyes, appearing adept. He had to admire her calm even as his mind raced with the possibilities.

A mental invitation reached out to him to join their many minds. He was not new to mind-meld, having trained all his life on his native planet, Qontaq, to amplify powers with others, but the force of this connection jolted him.

Yanda had a keen sense of Shalt, subsuming the circle of minds she had entered in that all-encompassing communal circuitry. Then Shouma joined them from the Sarsefi, and the energy of the rest became backdrop. "Remember when we worked with Bonden and Dele to shield the stone shards you drew across the universe?" Shouma asked.

"I do," Yanda responded. She would never forget that profound experience, lying on Shalt's surface, finding and drawing each piece of The Stone—every sliver of that unique essence—until all coalesced back into the massive and marvelous moon of Terlond, the Elf Stone of the Neyna.

"You must help me do that for our ships. The Lark is locked onto the Sarsefi so we should be able to shield both as one," Shouma went on.

Yanda could tell that all the mind-meld had heard and understood the imperative Shouma outlined. Bonden and Dele joined, prepared for a momentous protective act to help the ships safely under the Rotoul dome before attack by the swiftly approaching Blaz ships.

Hovering on the periphery of powerful mind-meld circle, Ilan sent his thoughts into the AI program he favored without opening the Mons. At the same time, he locked onto Tlalit in space and they shared grids, and Ilan moaned inwardly as they identified locations of hostile ships approaching the Lark and Sarsefi.

With some relief, he found that Sonda ships—of Shouma's powerful people on the planet Elznap they'd recently departed from—tracked the enemies as well, keeping a distance.

Qontaqian and Allandian star vessels but their allegiance was not clear. There were those on both planets who'd allied with their enemies in the past—the Blaz.

This could be a bloody battle. Ilan let the information seep first into Yanda's mind. She could decide when to share it with the powerful circle where she sat

He knew she had conveyed it when the mind-meld wrapped their protection around the linked ships, the Sarsefi containing so many they loved, and the Lark, holding Merne's son, and Yanda's past lover. Ilan had never met him and dreaded the moment that happened.

The elven circle that could hold a dome of protection over its magical forest also now obscured the allied ships from detection. The Sarsefi jumped into hyperdrive, blinking out from the grid momentarily, reappeared at new coordinates, out and in again, entering Terlondian atmosphere, speeding toward the Neyna dome.

The residents of Rotoul—adult elves and the few children of their clan—gathered on a hillock as Yanda and Ilan soared down from Vashal. Seiti and Zami stood with Arsat watching the Sarsefi and Lark take shape in the night sky. The ships drifted through a temporary opening in the dome's invisible membrane. Blowing fine dust in a cloud that fell before it reached the audience, the ships settled with only a low rush of sound.

A ramp lifted outward from the Sarsefi and three figures emerged. Yanda sent her sight close to see them more clearly. Her heart hammered as she made out Tenali, brawnier than most elves and not quite as tall as his mother, Merne. Tlalit followed mother and son.

"I'll never be an elf." Pressed to her shoulder, Ilan must have detected her racing heart. He let the thought seep into her mind like a pout. "Not even *half*-elf."

She elbowed him, though not hard. "You're Qontaqian. That's quite impressive enough." A phalanx of thoughts accompanied her words, about the mixed blessings of the elves in her life.

"And the Stones?" he thought back to her, his chest a warm presence. "They too have harmed your life. Stole you from your daughter. Ruined your surgeon career."

Was he jealous of the Stones as well? "We both know there was no safety for me on Alland." In that instant, she realized this was true. An imminent end to her life as esteemed doctor in the major city of Alland had been inevitable. That it was precipitated by the Stone's call was immaterial in some ways. A tightness she'd held ever since being abducted away from her daughter years before eased in her at this insight, courtesy of Ilan.

Suddenly Zamani gripped Yanda's shoulder. "Your daughter is calling to the Blaz, announcing our location."

Elven eyes turned toward her as shock registered. She felt the instant closing of the dome, as she helped hold the mind-meld's power.

"They would have guessed anyway, that Seiti was brought here," Ilan said, defending the young girl.

Merne appeared in front of them with a flash. Her hands shot out to Seiti's shoulders and the girl slumped. Yanda cried out, catching her daughter before she hit the ground. Merne snatched the unconscious girl from Yanda's arms and disappeared.

"She'll take her to the Sarsefi," Yanda shouted. Lifting Zami, she snapped out of sight.

Just in time, Ilan grabbed her arm and arrived at the Sarsefi with them to see Merne disappearing into the ship. Ilan scooped Zami from Yanda and the three ran after.

"Damn those Blaz!" Ilan exploded insults with every step as the chambers closed behind them on their swift dash to the lift, heading for the Flari pool on the top floor. They knew that was where Merne would go.

"I know she had to stop Seiti by knocking her unconscious but jeez...that was harsh." Yanda panted, out of breath and stunned.

They burst through the door into the spa room in time to hear Merne yelling to Soni, "She wasn't clear. She's signaling...We didn't clear her completely. We should have—"

"I was afraid you needed to do a deeper scan with your AI," Yanda said to Ilan.

"We know." Soni adjusted settings on the pool she'd invented.

The transparent isolation cube still stood near the wall of the spa room. Merne was inside, Seiti draped unconscious on her lap.

Bonden stared in, her strong hands clenched. She'd been part of detecting any taint left in the girl's body or mind.

Chin paced, long soldier legs stomping loudly. "I might know what it is," she muttered. Born on Blaz, Chin had been held captive with Yanda and eight other fems by Krid—cruel, greedy mage, collector of objects and living sentient beings with powers. Trained on Blaz to be a deadly fighter, she was a woman of few words.

Yanda drew close. Had she heard her right? She stopped the brawny woman who towered over her, with her thatch of rough-cropped tawny hair. "Chin, did you say you know—?"

Chin's hand encompassed Yanda's shoulder in a tight grip. "I think it's... but I don't know how... it's the...it could be...something they do...your head." She slapped her own temple with the flat of her large hand.

Yanda gripped Chin's forearm, trying to slow her down. "I don't understand what you're saying. You think you know something that might be in Seiti's mind? Come tell Soni and Shouma."

Though a highly trained female soldier, Chin followed, meek and unsure as a child. Guilt and misery at her connection to the Blaz, her intimate knowledge of their heinous ways, was written all over her face as she tried to explain her suspicion.

Yanda lay on her fluffy loft bed, groggily rubbing her eyes as the rich scent of fresh baked goods penetrated her senses. She could not turn back into her pillow, back into sleep; wafting olfactory delights pulled at her. She struggled out of blankets, and it hit her, a punch in the gut. Seiti was not out of danger. And she was not in the treehouse. She lay on a pile of pillows in the isolation cube. She drew

Seiti to her and kissed her cheek, thinner than she remembered. Was she still unconscious? The girl's breathing seemed steady and untroubled. Yanda dared not wake her.

Through the clear plaz wall, Ilan, looking sleep-deprived, in a camp chair, hunched over his keyboard, tapping in code and munching on a roll.

She pressed her hand to the pad by the exit and stepped out, immediately spotting rich tan buns in a tray, glistening with buttery glaze. She quietly shut the door and made her way to the warm rolls. Biting into one, she savored the rich, nutty flavor.

The night came back to her in all its misery: hours spent searching for what might be detected in her daughter's mind, left by the Blaz.

"We'll have to find what triggers Seiti's unconscious communication to her Blaz minders," Chin had said, endeavoring to explain the grueling years she'd spent working to remove the conditioning of her childhood and teen years on Blaz, once she escaped. "It will take time. It can't be done in an instant."

Now Yanda dropped to her knees to look at what Ilan worked on. As expected, he was researching how to untrain mind-conditioning.

Many around the spa room were stirring, on camp beds, probably woken by the scent of fresh-baked morning buns.

"Did the cube prevent her from sending any more signals to the Blaz?" Yanda whispered. "Can you tell?"

"All her signaling stopped when Merne knocked her...put her to sleep," Ilan said, trying to be reassuring.

"That's good. Do we know a psychologist?" Yanda sipped steaming *kran*. "Maybe hypnosis would work."

Tlalit entered, followed by Merne. "Decru," they said at once.

Tlalit spoke reverently of the elder elf who lived in the labyrinth of caves behind Shalt. "He can detect and remove any influence. He misses nothing."

"Will he come here?" Yanda asked. She wanted to get Seiti out of the cube as soon as possible.

"We've called to him for help," Merne said. "Do you like the blalims?" She broke open a bun, breathing in the warm yeasty aroma. "Elven bakers brought them to us moments ago."

"Heck, yeah. They made my dream mind perceive I was in a treehouse, in a nest soft as down." Yanda munched on another bite with relish.

"Mushroom flour," Merne explained. "This is from the *speradi*, a most comforting fungus."

Ilan grinned at this information, finished his roll with one large bite, and returned to reading.

A message penetrated Yanda's mind, sharp and clear. Unmistakably Decru. "Come to me." The next instant, Yanda stood in the finely furnished hall of the eldest Neyna elf. Seiti lay on a lavish couch of dark purple, with forest green brocade edging.

Yanda had been in this chamber only once before, when Decru had been part of the final operation bringing Shalt's shards back from across the universe. At that time, Zamani had explained these rooms in the caves were hundreds of years old; his father Garn, who'd lived four hundred years, had occupied the same den before him.

"Sit." Decru gestured toward a chair with plump stuffing. As she remembered him from before, he wore robes, vest, and pants of intricate design, cloth overlapping with embroidered folds. "I shall wake her. No harm will come to her." The old elf pulled a quilt over Yanda's sleeping daughter, then pulled a stool carved like tree roots close and sat.

"But—"

"There is no worry of her calling to the Blaz from here. My room is secure," Decru added as if he read her thoughts.

Yanda settled where directed and took a quick look around the shadowed spaces. Float-globes gave low lighting and warmth. There was an ancient feel to Decru's chamber with its carved columns and deep recesses holding objects of unguessable use or meaning. The only door she saw was of dark wood, carved in forest scenes, though there could have been more doors at the back where mysterious curtains of rich velvety fabric hung at intervals.

The elder elf reached a bony hand toward Seiti. Intense energy sizzled in the air. Yanda recalled the force when he'd taken her hand before. It had been painful at first but she'd been changed by it, given a new vitality that had never entirely dissipated from that original charge.

Seiti's eyes opened and she scooted to sitting, smiling.

Yanda was grateful Decru's energy seemed to have been softer for her daughter.

He turned to Yanda. "I want you here to know I will not harm her. But I cannot include you in this process. It could be damaging to both of you. After, I will share any part of it you want to know."

Why had Shouma not found all, like she did with Tenali? Had the Blaz more wily methods? Or was it easier to hide them in a child's mind. Either way, Shouma had missed things. Yanda's stomach tightened as for the first time she perceived fallibility in the older woman she'd come to know as all-powerful.

"No one is all-powerful," Decru said, and she knew this time that she'd let him help himself to her thoughts. "Tell me about this previous process with the consummately skilled Sonda, Shouma." His voice had a rich timber, like old tree roots speaking.

Yanda described the process she'd been part of both with Zamani's grandson, Tenali, and with her own daughter.

"May I?" Decru stood, with the help of an elaborate walking stick, and stepped to her. He set the stick aside where it stood obediently, hovering mid-air, and pressed his hands to Yanda's temples.

She closed her eyes and let him into her mind. She had nothing to hide—and figured it would do no good to try anyway.

Seiti, meanwhile, watched them with calm curiosity. She had not yet spoken. Yanda wondered about that but drew her mind back to the hands through which he seemed to penetrate to her very soul.

After a long moment, Decru drew away. "That is most helpful. I now know much more, also where to seek." He returned to his stool and lay his stick aside. "May I have your hands, child?" He held his out, palms up.

Seiti willingly pressed hers to his. Yanda's heart clenched as she prayed this elf could be thorough, but gentle. Seiti's eyes drifted shut, but a smile lingered on her lips and did not leave.

CHAPTER

3

Yanda dangled her legs on the side of a deck high in the elven forest. Sun filtered through the forest's leafy boughs.

Ilan, just inside the treehouse, focused on his Mons screen, feet propped on a toadstool-shaped ottoman.

Zami was teaching Seiti to rise through the air high enough to grab a vine and swing through the forest. Though there was a six-year difference in age, the two laughed and giggled like old playmates.

"Swimming hole?" Yanda called to them.

"Now?" Zami's eyes shone as he swung up onto the platform.

Seiti followed, more awkwardly, catching herself on a rope handrail to pull onto the platform.

"Yes, let's go now. You have your first afternoon lessons with Tlalit." Yanda pushed to standing.

As they followed the path to the pools, the kids running ahead, Ilan asked, "What's Tlalit teaching them anyway?"

"Techie stuff, of course."

"You think she knows more than I can teach?"

Did it have to be either/or, Yanda thought, turning back to him and taking his hand, his gold-red hairs catching sunlight. "Of course not. But they'll have fun learning about the workings of the ship."

"I suppose Tenali will be there, too." Ilan nudged her forward to keep up with the kids.

So that was it. Ilan couldn't stop grilling her about Tenali. Now, his nemesis was on the same planet. She realized she hadn't seen her former lover at all in the night while she stayed in isolation with Seiti.

She and Tenali had been intimate, briefly and stormily. Their connection was like none she'd experienced. Half-elf, half-man, he, too, knew nothing of his real father. His sense of abandonment was different from hers but they had related to each other's pasts. His mother, Merne, obviously cared deeply for him, but bhe'd been raised by the elven clan, and most of all, his grandfather, the Neyna leader, Zamani.

Yanda hadn't told Ilan the details of their intimacy, but she suspected he sensed the intensity of it. The fact that this profound affair had come about even when she knew Tenali was her abductor, had given her over to Kridenit, to his imprisonment and rape, irked Ilan. Maybe enraged him. He couldn't understand how she forgave him. The fact that twice Tenali had risked his life to save her, had pursued finding her daughter, did nothing to assuage Ilan's suspicion, even hostility toward the other man.

"Would you like to teach them, too?" Yanda asked Ilan.

He was silent a moment as he ducked under a flowering bough. "We could teach each other," he said after some thought. "They could both teach me a lot."

Yanda grinned at him. "Me, too." She ran forward as the kids disappeared around a bend in the path.

The pools of Rotoul had been a fecund delight when Yanda, her then infant son, and the other nine fems, had first arrived, escaped from Krid after a year and half of captivity in the toxic city of Dondar.

Now Yanda shared the sunshine and sublime waters of this land with Ilan. He stripped to shorts and waded in. Zami and Seiti were already splashing toward deeper water. Zami dove, a high arcing leap. Seiti watched, admiring, then waded carefully deeper. Yanda didn't know how well Seiti swam. Had they taught her at Tiklet?

Yanda had worn a Neyla bodysuit perfect for swimming. There was nothing like the clothes that became part of her sea-creature body when she transformed to *lanten*. She wouldn't do that now. Climbing along rocks at the water's edge, she returned to a pool she'd frequented during her previous time there. Small and protected by high walls, it gave her a moment of privacy for thought. She dove deep and shot up out of the water. Her body held some of the muscle memory of the *lanten* state even when not in it.

Who knew how long the task hanging over Yanda would take, or even if it was possible? But one did not ignore the request of the two Great Stones of the Neyna and Neyla elves. Besides, she thought this would be her chance, at last, to meet her actual parents of the mysterious Xentu clan.

First, she would have to see the situation with Seiti solved, make sure she was out of danger and not a threat to them all. They would have to resolve the warring factions that threatened planets where their loved ones lived.

Coming up from a long swim underwater, Yanda saw Ilan standing on a rock wall, hands on his hips, gazing at her.

"I thought you wanted us to swim together," he called.

"I'll meet you back with the kids." Yanda pointed, then aimed for a submerged rock tunnel giving onto the main pool. She shot out on the other side, heading toward Zami.

Noticing her right away, her son laughed and dove deep to meet her. They arced out of the pool together.

Ilan watched with Seiti from the shallows.

Vatu called into her head. "I can't believe you're swimming without me!"

Soon nearly all their friends from the Sarsefi appeared by the small lake. Mnenu had already left for his sea home of Zotoul or he would have been first down there. Yanda found she missed him.

They all looked ecstatic to get off the ship and join them in a paradisical vacation, however short. The threat of war still loomed. The Blaz could easily surmise their location on Terlond though they'd have to get past the military presence around Terlond's atmosphere. Neither their hideout under the Neyna dome, nor the planet they'd just left—Elznap, domain of the powerful Sonda culture— would be easy to penetrate.

Yanda swam with Zami on her back like a baby otter while her mind traveled to other worries. Tlalit had come across the insidious news that Krid had been the highest bidder to buy her daughter. *Buy her*, as a child-weapon. Wouldn't she be the hallmark of his prize possessions. Yanda's stomach churned.

"Mommy? You okay?" Zami brought his soft cheek against hers over her shoulder.

He must have caught her livid thought of Krid.

"I'm fine. Sorry my thoughts aren't staying on this beautiful place we're in." She climbed onto a low flat rock and brought him onto her lap. "Your mama has a lot to worry about."

"You're thinking about Seiti?"

"You clever boy." She ruffled his brown-green curls. "A little bit about Seiti. We've made powerful people mad getting her from where she was."

He nodded sagely, then rubbed a leaf-shaped ear that dripped glistening water drops.

"You swim out and I'll send bubbles."

He giggled and shot out across the water, turning to see. He'd finally taught her how to make float globes. She bounced one out and he arced from the water to catch it.

Vatu crawled onto the rock next to her and they hugged. It was good to be back in the outdoors together. Vatu took a turn sending bubbles. The rest joined them and played. Ilan lifted Zami, then Seiti out of the water to catch balls. Shouma sent out a volley of rainbow bubbles from shore.

With others taking her play duties, Yanda rested her back against a curve in the rock and gave more thought to Krid. Certain controls hampered his movements, according to Tlalit, but clearly he worked around them for he was able to bid on a humanoid. He must once again be obtaining slaves.

Born on a water world, Vatu was the best of swimming companions. The blue Mingal female of delicate stature, head nubs now cerulean, had aquatic abilities equaling salamanders and dolphins. She dove off the rock and made her sinuous way underwater, then shot high, sweeping both kids with her. They squealed and Zami dove from her. Seiti stayed with Vatu, enjoying an eight-foot rise into the air, to be brought back down for a gentle plunge followed by a long glide.

Ilan joined Yanda on the flat rock and they watched the kids with Vatu.

"Want to see the hot springs?" Yanda asked.

A series of pools grew increasingly warm until the lowest gave a good hot soak. She scrambled to that one and crawled in.

Ilan plunked down next to her, his bulk raising the level of the water above her chin. She laughed spluttering as he pulled her into a languid hug.

They'd never finished any of their near kisses. Something had always come up, as it did now.

One who had not joined them at the pool was Gisli. He communicated into her mind, "We have a lot of intel. We should meet tonight. Or sooner."

"Are you on the Sarsefi?" she asked.

"I'm in the bunker. The Stones are starting to rumble."

"They want their sister back," Beri joined in their minds.

"You guys should at least come enjoy a swim after all that ship time," Yanda said

Ilan nodded agreement and angled for another kiss.

"But how realistic is that?" Beri's voice in her head seemed like he was present next to her. He was not to be dissuaded into the sensual pleasures of Rotoulian pools. Not yet, anyway. Being an interstellar journalist, Beri tended to report truths no matter the time of day or night, the convenience or the judiciousness. He specialized in stories of powerful objects and had found himself in deep water trying to rectify the theft of at least one.

Yanda pulled out of Ilan's embrace with an apologetic face-scrunch. "I don't know. I have the feeling a lot is realistic with these Stones and our crew," she responded, including Gisli and Ilan in her mind-speak.

"They can't cram a moon into a planet that formed millions of years ago," Beri objected. "Do they want to put their sister in orbit around Terlond? Wouldn't that require approval of the universal law council or something?"

"I doubt it," Yanda said, though she wasn't sure why.

Ilan ran a tempting hand up her side.

"We should go back," she said to him. To Gisli and Beri, she said, "I'm bringing the kids to the bunker. Tlalit wants to start a little school in there."

"It wouldn't be the first," Tlalit said, joining their mind-meld.

Yanda had heard from Merne of the Neyna elves' long stay in the extensive underground bunker, under attack by Krid's father and other colonizers to obtain the Great Stone's powers. That was before they'd created the immense transparent dome that now protected their forest home.

Reluctant to leave the hot pool and stirred-up tingles in her body, Yanda climbed out and started down the hill.

From the shoreline, she called out, "Time for lessons!"

Like a porpoise, Zami scooted across the surface of the water to her. Seiti followed in neat freestyle strokes. So Tiklet *had* trained her in aquatic skills. Or the rich privileged family who hosted her. That revelation soured Yanda's stomach. She was supposed to be the mother, aware of her daughter's lessons, cheering her from the side of the pool.

When Seiti stood dripping before her at the water's edge, Yanda put her hands on her shoulders and Seiti was instantly dry. Her red-black hair sprang up in a cloud, then settled on her shoulders. She laughed, a delighted yelp of surprise. "How'd you do that?"

Yanda thought about explaining *lanten*—how she'd learned from Mnenu to become part sea creature—but it was too big a topic. "I learned from the sea elves. That's a bit of a story. I stayed with them for a bit, searching for you."

"That's how you got to know Mnenu?" Seiti asked.

Yanda resisted glancing at Ilan. "It is."

Tlalit yelled into their minds, "Are you coming? We have two hours before dinner." She was calling from the underground bunker at the edge of the woods, with its multiple subterranean levels, comprising high tech, a gym and saunas, sleeping quarters, kitchen that could serve the entire elven community. Yanda'd never been to all the layers.

As she started up the path, she responded to Tlalit, "We're on our way," adding, "Seiti's in a swim outfit. We should go get changed at the treehouse—"

Ilan and her children trailed behind her as they filed up the path that seemed perpetually covered in blooms. Vatu and others straggled behind to see what this new school would be all about.

"We have loads of clothes here in the underground," said Merne, who'd clearly been listening to the mental conversation between Tlalit and Yanda. "We'll have some made for her, too."

Never having had a daughter, Merne seemed utterly transfixed by Seiti. She sometimes grew unnervingly controlling about her. Yanda had no doubt she would maneuver to keep her in Rotoul, along with Zami. But the female elf leader—daughter of Zamani—had saved the ten fems. She'd spent a year in the somewhat unsavory ghetto outside Dondar, plotting and preparing for their escape. Yanda found Merne's gold-brown cat eyes and forceful ways intimidating at times, but she mostly thought of both Merne and Shouma as the mothers she'd never had, raised as she had been by a cold, religious foster mother and closed-off foster father on Alland.

Yanda's mind leapt to the lessons Tlalit had suggested. She hoped they'd include knowledge of the elves' peaceful ways and amazing talents, nearly all involving nature in one way or another. Her thoughts wandered to other possible topics. She did not yet know the scope of her daughter's abilities. Could she see through walls and objects as Yanda did? She thought Seiti could change objects. That ability had started to appear before she was six, before both were abducted to different places. Yanda always regretted she'd never been home enough to know more about Seiti's growth, occupied with her surgery profession, living in a high-rise apartment in Skarth, riding the train home on weekends. If she was honest, once she'd escaped the weird home of her upbringing, she'd avoided it, yet she feared bringing Seiti to the city. Yanda's face scrunched with the irony. *Fat lot of good that did.* In the end, danger had found them.

Reaching the long low curve of the bunker roof lined in solar panels, they started down a stairway into shadow.

CHAPTER

4

Yanda enjoyed watching Seiti who marveled at the sights, sounds and smells of her first celebratory elven dinner. Every meal with the woodland elves seemed like an event but that evening, elf lights—bits of moss that glowed and sparkled from natural sources—festooned the trees, twinkling with magical sparkles. Ethereal sounds drifted from elves with musical instruments on a knoll. Yanda noticed Dele in their midst.

As they took their seats, Seiti studied the dishes along the tables that stretched the length of the large meadow. Yanda spotted Mnenu at the next table, returned from his Neyla clan in the undersea city for this gala affair. His eyes caught hers with a storm of mental energy, and he smiled. The sea elf already looked healthier than when on the ship, his skin the tones of lichen green, moss and jade.

Yanda searched the other guests among the residents of the forest community and felt an intense, familiar energy. At last, she spotted Tenali two tables over. He had not come to greet her on the Sarsefi. Now his gaze bore into her, but when she returned his look, his eyes darted away. Her heart raced and cheeks heated.

"Do you want the *takla deets*?" Ilan offered her a platter.

She loved the sauteed mushrooms with delicate crisp filagree breading and took a helping.

Ilan examined her face. He'd clearly sensed her reaction to finding her former lover gazing at her. Their arms brushed and she was acutely aware of a change in his breathing and temperature.

She smiled her thanks, wishing they weren't quite so attuned to one another. She took *takla deets* for Zami and Seiti's plates, then passed the platter on. With the three-pronged fork-spoon elven utensil carved from a light wood, she played with her food—a mound of cooked grains under sauce that drifted to her nose was mouth-watering. But she couldn't seem to bring a bite to her mouth; her stomach too keyed up. She wanted to run to Tenali and throw herself into his arms, to hold him, her body pressed to his, hearts beating as one. She hid these thoughts the best she could but Ilan was very hard to hide from. Since danger still hovered over the Neyna community and their guests, all ate with quiet chatter, the music subdued. The atmosphere matched her own torn sensibilities.

She was almost relieved when, delicious chocolatey pudding consumed and small gifts passed around, they rose as one to retire for the night.

Surreptitiously she watched Tenali move away from his table, in the opposite direction, his mother striding shoulder-to-shoulder with him. She thought he glanced her way but the trees quickly obscured them.

Yanda followed Chela, Shouma, and the others of their

group, tied forever, it seemed, from their collective captivity, moving through the woods toward their guest accommodations. She envied the sense of belonging she would have had in their midst and wished in ways that she and the kids still stayed with them in the larger treehouse. But she had her girl, and Zami. She rested an arm around Seiti's shoulders and a hand on Zami's head, playing with his curls. He hugged her leg. Ilan walked close behind.

When Yanda had read to her children and tucked them in with kisses, she climbed to her loft bed above their level. She read under a small globe light until her lids drooped. After she'd extinguished the light, she heard her kids voices in conversation.

"Why you go there?" Zami asked.

"I didn't have any choice," Seiti responded.

"Yes, you did. You had a choice to go to Blenin."

Yanda was astounded that Zami knew those details about his sister's past.

There was silence. Did Seiti resist answering? Did she hate to think back to that time? Or was there another reason for the hesitation?

Bedding rustled as though one of them flopped over. Yanda was tempted to look but didn't want to stop the conversation.

"Well, a lot happened," Seiti explained at last. "Someone came up to me on my walk home from school and said my mom was gone from the planet."

Yanda thought she heard Zami's quick intake of breath.

Seiti went on, "He said I shouldn't tell anyone yet, but he could help me find her."

"What was his name?" Zami asked.

Yanda held her breath. She hadn't had the nerve to pry into Seiti's experiences. After all, Yanda carried the burden of guilt. She was the reason...she wouldn't go there. Not now. She listened.

"His name was Arc. I learned that later."

Yanda gasped a quick silent intake of air she hadn't realized she held. She expected it to be Jelat.

"I know Arc," Zami said. "He seems nice. He helped you go to that moon where the Blaz took you away?"

Rustling. Was Seiti shaking her head?

There was no more talking. Breaths became even. Were they asleep?

After the conversation between her kids, she'd felt uneasy and nowhere close to sleep. Passing through the main room of their treehouse, she'd found Ilan still up, on his computer.

"I'm going for a walk," she said to him.

"Want company?" he asked.

"Not just now. Can you keep watch over the kids?"

"Yes, I can."

Yanda dropped into a chair next to Tlalit, whose face was lit only by screens that glowed in the otherwise dark subterranean rooms of the shelter's third level beneath the ground. "What did you teach them?"

Sensing Tlalit still awake in the bunker, Yanda headed down there. She was curious about the lessons, and wondered whether Seiti was truly clear after Decru's work. Since she'd met with Beri and Gisli, she'd missed Tlalit's teaching entirely.

It irked her that she could not be the one to assess her daughter. She wasn't only a capable surgeon. She'd been taught by Shouma to reach into distant minds and to explore deeply if necessary. She was led to believe that with her Xentu parentage, she should have astounding skills. It gave her expectations that were hard to live with.

"Remember, on Prokit's Moon?" Tlalit said, turning away from the bank of screens. "We were briefly in the underground city and I told you it's special, the rooms, the possibilities with other worlds. But we had no chance to dig in there."

"I do remember," Yanda said. "That undercity labyrinth was intriguing. We had to get out of there when someone attacked Bonden." Memories of the charming bungalow, the mattress in the basement, squeezed between Bonden and Ilan, flooded in. They'd fought a dark insidious presence in Bonden, as they did with Seiti now; Yanda hoped desperately that Decru had banished what was left. "I was sorry not to get more of a taste of your magical rooms."

"There's a world of learning possible in there. Nearly any question can be answered in those domains."

"Should we take Seiti there?" Yanda was willing to do anything to clear her daughter of taint or control.

"I don't think we'll need to. I did try something."

"Something?" Warning bells went off in Yanda's head.

"He's a genius, very big hearted. I trust him implicitly."

All these descriptors should have been creating trust but instead dread built in Yanda. "He. Who?"

"Hatch. He's built systems that one can set with specific source specs. We did a small test, in a game atmosphere, to see if any conditioning or traps still lurk in Seiti."

Yanda's back straightened to a ruler. "You should have talked to me. I don't want you to try anything else without consulting me."

The proud, confident Elf woman sagged. "Of course, Yandawi. What was I thinking."

Yanda thought she spotted a drop of moisture in Tlalit's wide, shapely eyes. She relented. "What did you find out?"

Tlalit eagerly leaned toward her elaborate set up of screens as well pop-out holographic ones angled on the wall. "We're finding a trail. I don't think it's from an evil entity, though. We may have removed all of that. Especially Decru did, but I'm sure Shouma also cleared a great deal. Of course, Soni and the Flari began the loosening of the Blaz grip."

Yanda knew very well the history of her daughter's treatments since they rescued her from Blaz. She didn't need this recounting. Why was Tlalit naming all this?

The Elf looked at her with a sidelong glance. "I know you know this. I'm thinking it through myself."

"Do you know more? Is this Hatch still tracking in my daughter's mind?" Yanda's acerbic tone rigidified her words. She was no-nonsense when it came to her children.

"No, no. It was just for a short while. He's withdrawn. I was monitoring, of course." Tlalit studied Yanda's face. "And I won't do more without involving you."

Suddenly Yanda felt very tired. She pushed out of her chair. "Okay, good enough." She kissed the still-seated elf-woman's peach and brown cheek. It felt like velvet to her lips. She touched Tlalit's shoulder. "Thank you. I do appreciate anything you think of to help clear Seiti, bring her back to her full self without any taint or influences."

"Of course." Tlalit patted Yanda's hand distractedly as she tapped keys, watching data streams.

Yanda climbed the steps out of the underground bunker and entered the night forest. Unsure of the location of their tree, she called to Ilan. He sent a float globe down the trunk of their treehouse.

"I should have thought to leave one of those," she said in mind-speak, smiling as she headed for it.

Next morning, as she and the kids tidied up, Yanda considered what Seiti might need. Her daughter had come to them with nothing. Vatu had given her lovely outfits, and now Merne had come up with more clothes from their elven storage in the shelter. Seiti liked them. Yet… Yanda remembered six-year-old Seiti. She'd collected so much over the years in the bedroom that Yanda occupied before her: books, figurines. As she grew, she'd managed to obtain arcane tools and obscure tech gadgets.

Yanda sat next to Seiti who was arranging gifts the elves had given to her the night before on her side table. "What do you need, sweetie. Is there anything you long to have? I haven't really thought to ask you."

An apology blazed in her belly for the years they'd been apart. Though they weren't her fault—not directly—they were compounded by the amount of time she'd been unavailable voluntarily, establishing her career as a surgeon. She couldn't carry that forever but didn't know when it would stop. Would there be time to heal?

Seiti shyly pulled something from under her pillow. It was an old-fashioned notebook of real paper. Yanda stared at it and touched the cover.

"I like to draw in this," Seiti said. "Sometimes I like to be off computer. But I probably should have a device pretty soon."

Yanda studied her daughter's face, then fingered the sketchbook. Paper made from natural sources—trees, plants of any sort—was a rarity. "Where in the Known Universe did you get this?"

Seiti fidgeted with an edge. "I didn't take it," she said.

Astounded, Yanda said quickly, "Of course you didn't. I didn't mean I thought you stole it." She got to her knees to look up into Seiti's face, now shadowed in a curtain of hair. More than anything, Yanda was determined that no misunderstanding should come between them.

Zami had grown quiet, lying on his bed listening, fingering his *woo-loo* toy.

Seiti whispered, "Tlalit gave it to me. Are you mad?"

Mad? Yanda thought, flummoxed. Why would Seiti think she'd be mad? Maybe from their session yesterday? Did she have some sense that Tlalit had gone behind her mother's back? That was something else they needed to talk about, Yanda realized. She brushed knuckles across her daughter's cheek. "I'm not mad. That's a marvelous gift. I wonder where she got it." She crossed her legs and leaned against the bed. "Let's figure out what kind of device you'd like to have."

"I like your ENAC," Seiti said.

"Oo. That's...let's consult with the IT team." ENACs

allowed powerful AI and distance systems activities, greater than most.

Ilan came to stand in the doorway. "Advanced taste this young lady has. Good choice though. There are attractive ones, lighter weight, easily portable." With a glance to Yanda, he reassured her they could set it up safely.

"Attractive? I don't want a dumbed-down version." An edge had crept into Seiti's voice. "I don't mind if it's heavy."

Fear crawled into Yanda, sliding along her nerves, clenching her stomach. She slid an arm around her daughter's waist. "She's always been very good with tech. She'll want the best." Her eyes spoke to Ilan.

"Oh, I don't think the size reduces the capabilities in the ENAC." He took a seat on a stool near a desk, clearly excited to explore the virtues of computer models.

CHAPTER

5

Yanda, Ilan, and the children joined the community at tables in the large forest glen for lunch. They sat near Tlalit, Merne, Gisli, and Beri.

Ilan still had his mind on obtaining Seiti a smashing portable computer. "Should we go into Dondar to shop?" he asked the group.

"We can have one brought here," Tlalit said. "It's not a good time to be in the city."

"Of course." Ilan immediately remembered the safety of the elven dome.

This led to discussion of Yanda's meeting with Gisli and Beri the previous afternoon. "I'm afraid Alland may have joined force with Blaz," she said.

"They wouldn't disclose that alliance openly, would they?" Merne said. "I thought that was the main point, to never show they worked with them."

Yanda remembered her trip with Ilan into Skarth, invisible, to track down the ones who'd allied to put her daughter in Tiklet, Blaz's sinister school making weapons out of children with powers.

"Well, they're mobilizing forces. Do you think it's to fight them or to help them?" Gisli asked. Having been a soldier and received tactical training as IT, he would be strong in helping analyze the threat.

"Maybe they're going to see which way the wind blows," Ilan suggested. "Duplicitous bastards." His mind leapt to the original subject, or perhaps had never left it. "But I could go." He was eager to shop in Dondar. "No one's looking for me, per se."

Yanda caught his desire. At the thought of returning to the city of their long captivity, her stomach roiled. To see the Citadel again? A wave of thought carried through the minds of the Ten Fems sitting at the tables, and included Zami who was too close to them not to hear. He'd been born into that hive-mind.

"We'll have to return sometime to where we were held captive," Shouma said. "to process what we went through, and let it go."

"I suppose." Yanda chewed at a mushroom stick, inwardly resisting that notion. *I never want to see that place, or Krid, again.*

Seiti perched at the edge of Decru's couch. A borrowed cotton gown hung like sacking on her light frame. She fiddled with a thread hanging loose from fraying embroidered edges, and sang. What was the song? Not one Yanda had ever heard. Her hair tumbled over her shoulders in cascades as she stood up and walked, feet barely touching the carpet, as though floating. Like a ghost. Yanda didn't want to think of her daughter as a ghost. For too long, she'd been a phantom—an elusive image Yanda held, grasping at the vaguest hints of where she might be: a waif crossing a shadowy street, caught on a camera in an unsavory city, a cry and a vision speaking to her from an unreachable moon in Unknown Space, where no one could survive.

Now Seiti approached one of the deep alcoves and reached for an object on a pedestal. She rubbed off dust and beauty shone suddenly from smoky blown glass that glowed.

Yanda had not seen Decru before this. Like a plant whose leaves shift incrementally toward light, he seemed not to move yet turned toward her. Was he in another dimension where time behaved differently? His arm, a spindle, slowly angled in a gesture. His fingers chiseled the air soundlessly, inviting her closer.

Yanda woke. It was a dream, she realized. But so real, she could still almost taste it. She tried to recapture Seiti's song in her mind. It seemed the words held clues.

Below her, Seiti stirred. Yanda thought she hummed. She leaned over the edge of her loft to listen. Yes, Seiti sang words now that sent chills along Yanda's spine. Yet, try as she might, she could not make sense of them. Were they even universal language, Unla?

Before she could continue trying to process them, someone else's voice caught at her mind in a deep resounding tone, barely within her register of hearing. Ash-Don called, "She must stop."

"Who? Stop what?" Yanda asked, puzzled.

"It's not time yet. She must not repeat…"

Unsure what it meant but certain of the urgency, Yanda scrambled down the ladder and scooped Seiti into a hug. "Shhh," she said quietly, brushing back her daughter's hair which stuck with sweat to her forehead. "No need to repeat the song."

"Why not?" Seiti murmured sleepily, seeming about to sing again.

Yanda put a finger softly to Seiti's lips. "I think it's essential you don't, honey." She kissed the girl's cheek, the texture, the girl's scent still familiar despite their years apart. "Can you believe me?"

"He wants it sung."

Yanda's stomach gripped but she made herself say calmly, "Who, darling? Who wants it?"

Seiti's lips parted. Yanda sent a desperate call to Merne.

Instantly the elf woman stood in the room. Yanda shot her a thought. "Put her to sleep again." She dared not utter the words for fear they would stay in Seiti's memory.

Understanding, Merne dropped to her knees and lay a hand on Seiti's shoulder. The girl's head drooped to Yanda's lap, instantly out cold.

"She was singing, in my dream and then when I woke," Yanda explained in a whisper. "Ash-don got agitated and said it's not time, she mustn't sing it, as if it might summon something. Or someone. Then Seiti said… 'he wants it sung.' *He.*" Yanda shivered, remembering.

"But you have no idea who she refers to? You caught nothing in her mind?" Merne folded to a crouch.

Yanda shook her head.

Ilan peeked in from the next room. "What's happened?"

"I'll explain." Yanda said, resting a protective hand on Seiti's shoulder.

Merne hissed, "We need to get her to the others. Shouma or Decru. Or the circle at Vashal, maybe. Clearly nothing's worked yet." Then, aimed at Ilan, she said, "I thought you put some sort of tracking, some AI in her psyche." She tapped her lip as though pondering. "I thought Tlalit did, too."

Zami slept on through all this.

"We have to get Ash-don's help," Yanda said. "He knows something."

"We don't need to—" Merne started to protest.

"I do." Yanda tried to stand holding Seiti but plopped back down. Seiti was no longer six.

Ilan gathered the unconscious girl into his arms, lifting her to his six-foot-seven. "Can I come?" Seiti's head rested on his shoulder.

"You want to see the undersea city, don't you?" Yanda scrambled to her feet. She pictured turning *lanten* in front of him and wasn't sure she wanted to. "You could only be in the upper parts of Zotoul, you know. You couldn't come to the sea cavern with Ash-don which is where we need to go."

"You breathe underwater?" he asked her, voice bordering on facetious.

"We don't have time for this conversation," Merne said. "Are you thinking Ash-don can help with Seiti's mind?"

"I think he knows the entity calling to my daughter,"

Yanda said firmly. "And if he does, that may be the only safe way to wake her again."

"Why don't you ask him who he thinks is calling her instead of racing across the sea?"

Yanda didn't want to explain herself. "Take us, Merne." She sent a mind-call to Mnenu.

Yanda's toes curled over the stone ledge below the sea elf circle and she leapt into the water, without hesitation, Seiti in her arms. She could not fear. *Lanten* hit; she became a sea being, carrying her young with powerful strokes. Ash-don awaited.

She reached the sentient stone's side and crawled, instinct dictating how to maneuver her daughter in the grip of her sea-creature arm, until they both lay on the massive convex curve of rock.

Ilan watched from a deep crevice in the great sea cavern, waves pounding and echoing all around. He'd followed the woman he loved, unknown by the rest. He would not let her out of sight.

She had shifted, becoming suddenly brawnier, different. What had she done to earn this reward, to remove her humanity at will, to burst from her skin into some other being? What bargain had she driven for this skill of the sea elves? He ached to follow, to be granted such release from his human form. At the same time, he shrank from her change.

As she maneuvered, arms crouching in a salamander stance, he caught a sidelong glance and her eyes were a beast's, no longer Yanda's. He pressed farther into the crack in the wall.

"Tell me who made Seiti sing," Yanda rasped, in almost a growl. She was desperate. Her hopes now lay with the Great Stone to cleanse her daughter of the invasive influence.

"I did not say it was necessarily an adversary," the Great Stone intoned.

"Then what? Who is he? What did you mean by 'not yet'? And what can you do so that I can safely wake her?" Yanda curled to sitting, cradling Seiti in her lap, no longer noticing the cold wet rock beneath her. Not noticing that a council of elves had been arriving, seating themselves in the circle of high stone seats on the round rock shelf far above.

Ilan saw Mnenu climb to one of the seats that looked down upon the dramatic, watery sea cave where Ash-don dwelt. He envied the handsome, lithe elf man. Yanda seemed to choose only elves as lovers. Not a bulky red-haired man from Qontaq who stared at computer screens too often.

"Yandawi, we need our sister stone, Melcraf, now. But we must clear the martial presence throughout the universe first."

"Melcraf? Is that who wants Seiti to sing?" Yanda asked, her throat squeezing to an ache. She had searched so hard, worked so hard to get her daughter back. Now one danger after another threatened her. "How will we do that? Clear the universe of hostile ships?"

"They are not a problem in themselves. Melcraf can protect herself. In fact, she's the only dangerous one of us three moons."

"You speak in riddles." Yanda grew impatient as her daughter slumped, unconscious, a dead weight on her. "How would we make it safe to bring your sister moon across the universe? And who is 'he'? What is this song he wants Seiti to sing, and why 'not yet'?"

"Dawi, Dawi, settle yourself. This may take time."

Yanda drew a long breath and let it trickle out.

"Inside Melcraf is a center stone. Not another moon. Not a full..." Ash-don paused as if to gather thoughts. "Not like us. Maybe he. Maybe not. Another mind. Your daughter perceives, hears. Do you remember when we saw her dancing on Melcraf's surface?"

Yanda froze. That moment...that terrible moment when her daughter begged her to bring her back. And she couldn't. She was there only in spirit-travel. But then, so was Seiti. On a moon in Unknown Space without atmosphere. "Yes. I remember." She pulled Seiti closer to her chest.

"When you saw her dancing, she was still at school."

"I know that now," Yanda almost snapped.

"Melcraf and your parents were reaching out. And he. The interior one who makes the black smoke."

This was making some sense now but Yanda had to be sure. "My parents are on Melcraf?" Yanda asked. "But how? No one can survive—"

"There's a way. It's a Xentu secret. How to use the smoke."

"Why did the Qontaqians have it? They put it into Bonden." Yanda's head felt fuzzy. Overloaded. None of Ash-don's answers seemed complete. "I'm wearying," she said. All the answers she'd sought seemed within reach, yet she suddenly sagged in unendurable exhaustion.

"Lay Seiti flat to my surface. Please." Ash-don's voice burred with the last word, more vibration than voice, if he ever did use a voice.

With others in mind-speak she heard their voices, at least on some level. But the Stones? Sometimes she heard tones, other times she perceived the messages in her bones.

Gently she rolled Seiti to the wet rock surface, belly down, her night dress soaking up the sea spray. Yanda stretched out next to her daughter and asked the Great Stone, "May I touch her?"

"Yes, please do," Ash-don responded.

Yanda lay her arm over her daughter's back and let her head rest in the crook of her rubbery sea-creature arm.

"Melcraf," Ash-don called. "We hear you. You must not call to Seitawi yet. The way must be cleared for you to come. Let the child be for the moment. Tell Shevan not to make her sing. Not yet."

Yanda snuggled closer to Seiti, bringing her face to Seiti's cheek, pressing close to see what she could read in her daughter's mind. Merne had put her soundly to sleep, as in a spell, but now Yanda felt activity. Seiti had been drawn into the mind-meld of the Neyla circle. And they all felt the new presence, a profound resonance, sweet and at the same time ice. Melcraf. Yanda shivered but pressed in closer to better know this compelling essence better.

Her parents were in the mind-meld as well. All the answers. Right there. Something was familiar. Something was part of her, had always been…part of her. Her parents were in a space—underground, she thought—on the moon, Melcraf. The enclosure was filled with black smoke, the evil substance they'd drawn from Bonden, it seemed to her. Within the murky rough-hewn chamber, shadowy figures stood; she sensed they were her parents, though, like so often in the past, she could not make out distinct features.

"You've been hiding in Unknown Space?" she asked them. "What is this dark smoke that surrounds you?" Yanda said to the Xentu, her birth clan.

Her mother responded, voice familiar, yet as unknown as a lost dream, "We did not want this for you," Dal'an, her birth mother, responded.

Yanda hitched a sob, for all she'd lost, all she'd never had.

CHAPTER

6

From a hammock, Yanda and Seiti looked out from the treehouse, across woods to a meadow stretching toward low hills. The elven swing caused them to sit into each other.

Yanda loved the warmth of her daughter pressed to her. She let her head rest against the back edge, eyes drifting shut. Sun speckled on them, the orange sun of Terlond.

Seiti didn't seem to remember anything about the night before. Yanda was glad. In ways. The Circles, the Stones, and the bunker were gearing up to make the universe safe. Yanda would be called when she was needed.

"We played in a field," Seiti said.

Yanda's eyes popped open.

"I liked when we went to it. It wasn't really *outside*—it was in the dome with the school—but it looked like there was sky above us."

Yanda's heart raced. Calmly she asked, "What did it smell like?"

Seiti's dark amber eyes peered at her a moment. "Mm. Grass." She breathed as if bringing back the memory. "We played a game. Like soccer. I remember my friends shouting in all their various accents, our crimson uniforms, the oblong ball. Half wore sashes, jade color, out in the faux sunshine. I don't even know what Blaz sun looks like. When we went between the domes, the windows had a dark tint so it always looked like night."

Yanda remembered riding in the transport vehicle, invisible and tiny, hidden in a compartment when they saved Seiti. She'd been focused on the girls and their minders.

"What were your friends' names?" Yanda asked.

At moments like this, she thought maybe it was okay, the school her daughter had been taken to. Maybe it was healthy enough, like other schools.

Then Seiti went on, ignoring her question about names, "But when we got back from sport, they showed us videos of our performance and made us try to beat our times, talked about force, velocity, speed, achieving our height of perfection. Economy of movement. It became painful and grueling and wrecked it." Seiti was silent a moment. "Then we remembered."

Yanda's heart sank with the proof Tiklet was making her daughter into a weapon.

"Remembered?"

"That we weren't there to have fun."

"Did they ever talk about what you would be doing when you left there?" Yanda asked, deciding it was time to speak directly.

"Oh, yeah, we got all the propaganda. We would serve a valuable purpose. We were being trained to be the best so that ya-da-ya-da-ya-da. Peace, freedom…"

"And you knew — some of the other girls knew — it was a charade?" Yanda asked.

"A few of us dared to talk. We had ways. But it was dangerous. We — saw what it could mean if caught."

"You saw what?"

At that moment, Shalt called to her. "We will begin. You and Seiti must come to me."

Yanda wanted to continue this conversation with her daughter. What had they been threatened with? Well, of course, it would be dire. Blaz was not a joke.

Seeing the elegant homes from the transport when they'd stolen Seiti back, she'd let herself imagine it might have been softer, an exception to the cruelty and wickedness of the rest of the planet.

Decru called into her mind then, "Are you ready? I will bring you directly to my rooms."

Yanda's mind flashed to the dream she'd had in Decru's chamber. Was it important somehow to this moment? She took Seiti's hand. "The stones want us to help now."

"Help bring Melcraf and your parents? My grandparents?" Seiti asked, and her eyes gleamed with eagerness.

Or was it something else?

Was she compelled toward some unknown fulfilment?

"Yes. Well, maybe not yet. At least the clearing of the universe. I'm not sure what that might entail. We're basically going to try to remove the threat of war."

Seiti nodded solemnly. "I've been prepared for that. I might be able to help."

Yanda searched her daughter's face. Prepared? She couldn't get all the answers now.

To Decru, she said in mind-speak, "We're ready."

Instantly they stood in Decru's chamber with its rich

color tones and ancient carvings. Shouma waited there as well.

Decru took their hands, one of Yanda's and one of Seiti's. "Do you remember when I prepared you to help Shalt the last time?" he asked Yanda.

She nodded, remembering the jolt.

"I believe most of that strength remains in you," he said, eyes half-lidded.

She felt his presence in her, traveling through her veins and muscles, enlivening her cells. There was no pain.

Decru again faced Yanda, powerful eyes connecting with hers in that all-encompassing way of his. "This process will ease the attunement when you come in direct contact with Shalt. Shouma is joining us to help make sure nothing errant comes into young Seiti, or leaves from her. Is that satisfactory to you?"

"Yes. Of course. Who better than the two of you?" Yanda asked.

Decru bowed, hand to his chest. "I am honored by your trust."

Shouma faced Decru and took their other hands. The four vanished, appearing on Shalt's wide curved surface. As before, the stone glowed warm scarlet under their feet.

Further away, the smooth agate-like moon turned ice blue, dark indigo beneath.

Perhaps it was her imagination but once she lay prostrate on Shalt, her clothes seemed to disappear.

The four of them stretched on their stomachs, Decru between Yanda and Seiti, Shouma on the far side of the girl. Yanda wished she could be touching her daughter but she cared more that two such powerful beings surrounded Seiti and monitored her.

Tlalit, Merne, Mnenu and the rest joined into their minds. Yanda detected the Stones' Circles as well.

She touched her daughter's mind. "You're okay?"

"It's awesome," Seiti whispered.

"Kiss, kiss," Yanda conveyed.

Seiti returned them.

And then another mind swam into Yanda's consciousness.

Tenali.

To have side conversations during a large mind-meld was challenging. But the hive, extending from Rotoul across the sea to Zotoul, still worked on settling into a shared vibration with the stones.

Tenali's voice brushed her briefly. "I've had no time with you."

"Soon?" Yanda asked, keeping their connection as private as she knew how, with all those other minds present in hers and his.

"Yes," was all he responded before the mind-web ramped up into energy so profound, it was all Yanda could do to press her hands to the stone and hold on.

Screens filled her mind, images out in the universe. This was from Tlalit and Gisli. Ships hovered in space near Alland, Terlond, and other planets known to Yanda, even Mingal, Vatu's beloved watery planet, bright turquoise, with a ring of small moons.

Then dark, thick as a shadow's underside, filled her mind and sight. Yanda thought she might suffocate. She struggled to breathe in a tunnel filled with goo.

Had she slipped away from the mind-meld?

This was no storybook that she could close and walk away from. She could not mitigate the pure horror.

This could not be where her parents dwelt, though she suspected it was. No, not this tar-like atmosphere.

I must be only spirit here, she said to herself. *I should be able to leave. But how?* She was compelled then to walk forward. A bridge stretched in front of her. Stepping onto it, she looked down. Something moved beneath it. Not water. Did it move or did the bridge sway with her on it?

A voice came into her head. Or did it fill the cavern? She gripped the bridge's guardrail. What was it made of? Not wood or any texture she'd touched before. She rubbed it, clinging desperately to anything solid; her children were lost from her. She could not detect Shalt or any familiar mind.

The voice began to sing. Though the language was unfamiliar, she understood enough to know the lyrics posed riddles. Its owner expected answers. No amount of concentration brought clarity. Was it a dream? Even so, something seemed to be at stake: she would soon have to answer correctly or all would be lost. Yanda tried to call out but the voice stopped her. Both syrup and vinegar poured into her mind; reaching the others was impossible.

Slowly she realized the voice came from what moved under her, passing beneath the bridge. It had to be massive, the width a flowing river, continuously sliding past.

Somehow she found her voice. "I don't like this," she snapped, then shouted, "I don't like this!"

A tenuous filament of awareness entered her mind. Ilan. She grabbed at it as a lifeline. That's all it took, the mere spark.

"I couldn't find anyone. I…" She breathlessly tried to communicate.

"You're here. You're okay," Ilan assured her.

"I'm sorry I wasn't helping. I was pulled…"

"Your presence is all we need," Decru said then.

She became aware of her body on the hard stone that warmed to her presence. "What's happening? What can I do?"

"The stones, and all your allies—all the powerful minds—have established a presence on every hostile ship," Decru explained while holding the mind-meld, as they all did.

"I'm running AI throughout the systems as well," Ilan said. "We know who is acting on our behalf now. Alland has retreated."

Yanda could see what he was seeing, in his mind. He'd joined the IT team in the bunker. "But what's being done?"

So as not to overwhelm her, Ilan and Decru trickled light streams of awareness. Rather than information, Yanda saw images and knew data as it sat in their minds: they were doing whatever it took to make the enemy ships retreat.

"Like what?" Yanda prompted.

Tlalit's voice joined the others in her mind. "Cut off oxygen. Change anti-grav settings. Send false messages. Tangle communication. Gisli is very clever at that one." She chuckled.

"And it's working?" Yanda asked.

"Oh, it's working," Ilan said.

Yanda was silent a moment, then said, "I'm not sure about bringing Melcraf here."

CHAPTER

7

Yanda thought about the black serpent-river that wound its way through the moon Melcraf's interior. She would not describe it now and bring that terrifying essence into the mind-meld.

But she wanted to make sure they didn't go straight from clearing the universe to drawing the missing moon to Terlond.

Her words had been taken in by the entire meld, however. For some seconds, there was utter silence, though the sabotaging of the mission to re-capture Seiti continued.

Zamani's strong mental voice rang into their minds. "Once space is cleared and our stance known—that Seiti is under the protection of the Elves and the Sonda—"

"And the Xentu." Yanda's father spoke.

Yanda froze, attuning to a voice that meant too much to her, that she trusted little.

"And the Mingal," Vatu said. "I have checked and they are ready to help."

"And the Jejods," Aktat announced, "though we have smaller gifts to impart."

Zamani responded to these offers, "I thank you. You are all needed." He paused, then continued his original message, "Once this is achieved, we will meet before any other action. Yanda has new information."

Well, not really information, she thought. *I don't know what that was but I think it's related to the dark smoke.* She wanted to run this by Ilan. Of course, the ones who knew were her parents. But just now she longed to be wrapped in his warm arms with their amber hairs that arced. She wanted to be up in the treehouse with her children. "How close are we to finishing?" Yanda asked.

"You've been through something, child," Decru said. "I have some idea what. You and Seiti, go with Shouma and derive comfort. The hardest part—piercing the defenses—has been achieved with all our minds together in one force. You deserve to rest. Your girl did magnificently and should not be taxed any further at one time."

Yanda couldn't believe she'd been unaware of what Seiti was accomplishing. She would find out later. Right now, she was ready to accept Decru's reprieve.

When the three—Yanda, Seiti and Shouma—arrived at the ground-level door to the subterranean bunker, they were fully clothed, just as when they'd left their treehouses. Yanda grabbed Seiti into a hug and pulled her down the stairs. On the third level underground, Ilan turned at the sound of their footsteps as though he'd known they were coming.

Tenali sat further along the row of seats at the counter below banks of monitors. Yanda's heart raced to see him.

She turned back to Ilan. "Can you do what you're doing

from the treehouse?" she asked him, aware of Tenali's intense gaze.

"Yes, I'm sure I can. You must be exhausted." He stood and hugged her, not as he would if they were alone, a brief embrace.

She breathed him in and they dropped apart. She turned to Tenali. Their first greeting couldn't wait forever. She stepped to him, Ilan's and Seiti's eyes on her back.

Yanda reached out to Tenali. "It's good to see you."

"Nice to see you, too," he said, subdued, as he stormed her mind with thoughts. One stood out. "Who is this guy?"

"Let's catch up when things calm down," she said. She turned halfway. "Tenali, meet my daughter, Seiti." She put out an arm inviting her daughter forward.

Seiti came and shook Tenali's hand, studying his face, head tilted.

"And you've met Ilan?" she asked, assuming they must have introduced themselves.

Tenali put out a hand and Ilan took it. They shook briefly, then squared off, examining each other close up.

"I don't really know Ilan's role in all this, I have to admit," Tenali said. "Maybe you've told him more about me than vice versa."

This wasn't going that well.

Seiti leaned into her mom.

"I'm going to get this girl into bed. I think they'll call if they need us," Yanda said.

As Ilan, Seiti, and Yanda turned to walk away, Tenali asked into Yanda's mind, "Staying in the same treehouse, are you? Playing house?"

What to respond? It had been months since they'd seen each other. Since, she'd been lovers with Mnenu. And now…she knew Ilan cared about her, had her back, was a big, loyal, warm haven. But she also had a hot wire close to her groin. Her stomach jumped flips at the feel of Tenali's hands. Her heart hammered with a sweet ache for him.

As Yanda, Seiti, and Ilan made their way through dark forest to their treehouse, the only noises they heard were a few nocturnal marsupials, a *jaja* bird swooping among high boughs, and intermittent voices, in laughter or settling sleepily.

Vatu responded to Yanda's mind-call that all was well. Zami slept.

When the three had floated up to their platform, they found Vatu in the bedroom. She'd made herself a comfy sleeping mound of cushions and quilts. A children's book lay open between her and Zami.

Vatu jumped out of bed to hug each. "It felt strange not to be with you this time," she said to Yanda.

"I know but I felt you there with us."

"Once Zami fell asleep."

"Thank you for being with him. I don't know what I'd do without you. What *we'd* do." Yanda thought she shouldn't say that. She should encourage Vatu to return to Mingal, to have her own life.

"I want to know what I missed," Vatu said, patting Yanda's cheek and stroking Seiti's hair.

Seiti said, "I'll get ready for bed." Her hair was mussed, her outfit wrinkled from hours of hard work in the mind-meld.

"Good idea," Yanda said, realizing she couldn't very well dress for bed with all of them in there. "I'll be right back." Yanda brushed a kiss to Zami's neck, hugged Vatu again, and pushed Ilan out. "Want something hot to drink?" she called as they passed through the living area.

"No thanks," Vatu answered. "I've had lots."

"Can we talk?" Ilan said, pulling at her arm.

"Let me bring us tea." Yanda popped into the kitchen.

He sat in bed, propped against pillows, tapping at his keyboard, as Yanda carried in steaming mugs. Handing one to him, she set the other on the far side and climbed in next to him. She'd never been in Ilan's bed, exactly. She rested her head on his chest, the warm cup against her, and told him about her time on the bridge, and about the smoke snake. It was hard to speak of it, especially her sense of helplessness as she found no one else's mind, alone in the thick black air. She was shaking.

He took the cup from her and set it by him, pulling her in closer.

When she'd finished what she could make sense of, he said, low and gentle, "You will need to show Shalt and Ashdon. Probably everyone. If you're concerned that Melcraf and this...being...aren't to be trusted, I mean."

Yanda pushed to where she could meet his eyes. "How could I tell that to the stones? This is the sister they've been wanting to be reunited with for millennia. Or *millions* of years."

"Maybe this dark river-snake being came when they lost contact with their sister moon," Ilan suggested.

"But Decru mentioned the singing."

"And that's who sings? The smoke river?" Ilan asked in a calm, reasoned voice.

"That's who sang to me on the bridge."

"The same as the one who sang to Seiti? Did you recognize it as the song you heard her sing?"

Yanda thought. "I do need help to understand. Shouma could work with the memory. Go right in there." She buried her head into his shirt and mumbled into his chest, "I don't want to be back there. What if it absorbs me again and this time no one can get me back?"

He rubbed her shoulder. "Do you trust Shouma? Or Decru? Either could take you."

Ilan got no answer.

Utterly exhausted, Yanda had dropped to sleep.

The next day, after a hearty morning meal, Yanda's legs were rubber as she sank onto the green couch high up in Vashal, where Tenali had had his memories examined for any presence of Krid. Always before, she had been an equal member of the great mind-melds. Now all eyes would be on her and her memories, Shalt's power circle in their stone seats one level above, a twin circle of powerful Elves across the sea in Ash-don's cave. Others were joining them as well, from the bunker and from treehouses.

Shouma sat near her head. Yanda twisted to see her in her priestess robe of jewel-toned satin stripes. Shouma patted her, encouraging her to lay still.

A punch in the gut proclaimed that instant when all the minds entered one space, merged in one vibrating energy. Only for an instant, Yanda hesitated, dreading going back to that influence, that being, immensely seductive and intractable, absorbing her into the aloneness.

Then Shouma splashed her mind with her own, dousing away the others. A yard away, Shouma's mind filled

Yanda's. Soft as velvet, she brought her down, down, into that experience of horror when first taken by the thing in the tunnel, stepping onto the bridge, seeing the endless slow movement below, that dark, smoky river that had a mind.

Somehow Shouma kept her feeling safe as the memory bloomed. This time, she was not alone.

The mind-meld waited quietly, stepped with her, gripped the railing, felt its texture. All heard the whispered riddles. Was it a whisper? She'd heard a voice, in Seiti's mind, and it was sweet. Could the black smoke turn sweet or sour at will?

Now there was no feeling of embarrassment as all heard and saw it with her. There was relief.

Suddenly, the voices of Shalt and Ash-don joined the moon-being, reciting the riddles. Complex sounds rumbled and grew louder. They sang together, the three. It was like a nursery rhyme they'd all said many times. Yanda's heart sped up. Now, instead of a demanding riddle, it brought laughter. Ash-don and Shalt were shaking with their stone-laughter. It vibrated in Yanda's bones.

When the amusement tapered off, Shalt explained, "It's a riddle, or a rhyme. It has no certain answer, or has several."

Yanda's chest ached, where just before, it had felt lightened. "Why did I feel like I had to answer?" *Oh, very well for you to joke,* she thought. *It wasn't funny at all, alone and not knowing the rhyme.* "Why did she pull me there, all alone, and say this rhyme to me?" Yanda felt petulant, and now slightly self-conscious that so many listened as she felt like crying.

"That's Melcraf. She's not bad," Shalt defended. "She

wants to teach you. Too quickly. She's very eager. She's been alone so long."

"That was Melcraf then? Who spoke to me? The dark smoke flowing under me?"

"It is part of her, yes," Shalt answered.

"Do you have parts of you like that? Other beings, other voices?" Yanda asked.

Ash-don and Shalt sent fluting sounds between themselves.

Shalt sighed, a mental breeze. "There is more for you to learn about us stones. But for now, let me assure you, Melcraf meant no harm."

"I didn't feel like I could pull away. I had no sense of my own volition, or of any others' presence in my mind," Yanda said, pouting, wanting the rest to understand what it had really been like.

"Our sister moon has been in Unknown Space a very long time. It is you, in your search for your daughter, who brought us back together. We have been apart—oh!—so many years. And without contact, she has perhaps forgotten that certain...hmmm...protocols should be followed. We will work with her."

"What about the Xentu? Haven't they been with her? On her, or in her?" Yanda asked, wondering if her parents had joined this meld. She could not detect them but thought they were able to hide.

"Ah. The Xentu."

"Yes. The Xentu. My parents. I've seen them in the dark smoke. I've sensed... Well, you saw them, too. When we saw Seiti on Melcraf. Of course, she could not be there. Her spirit danced there, called to me." There was silence. A dread filled Yanda, that this had all been one more sleight of hand. "Are my parents there only in spirit? Do they show me and others themselves in that dark smoke so we'll guess that it allows them to be in unknown space when really they're not there at all?" She waited again for an answer. "Do you even know?"

"I think we'll discover almost as much as you when Melcraf arrives in orbit around Terlond," Shalt answered.

Yanda gave a muffled groan and opened her eyes. She sat, letting the mind-meld drop away. She was afraid she would start bawling. As it was, she climbed from the couch and knelt, rested her head in Shouma's lap. Tears soaked into the flowing satin skirt.

CHAPTER

8

What *was true?* Yanda raged as she stomped down the hill into the woods, having left Shouma and the memory-dig behind, high on Vashal. She never knew the full story; those around her who claimed to care had more information than they divulged. Those who seemed most invested in her could be the most befuddling. Not Ilan. At least she didn't think so. But then, she had no idea what he hid from her.

She did not turn toward the treehouse where Ilan, Vatu, and the kids awaited her. Instead, she skirted the back side of the bunker, where clever screened pockets dropped a hundred feet allowing vined foliage to give off green light into subterranean atriums. She found herself on the mound where she'd first experienced the full force of Shalt, the moon-sized stone in a nearby massive labyrinth of caverns. Her booted feet took her down the slope, into the dark entrance to the caves.

But it wasn't the Stone she sought.

Could she reach Decru by foot? She'd only entered his ancient rooms being brought there in instant travel.

She crossed the fathomless vaulted cave's rough floor, boots crunching. Arriving at the thirty-foot wide hole, she gazed down at Shalt's icy blue surface, where she'd lain naked, pulling its Stone fragments from across the universe.

The immense cavern's dank, loamy smell brought her back to those first times when the Great Stone's powerful energy had shaken her nerves until they were ragged with tension. Now the vibrations warmed her, sending subtle heart palpitations.

"You're looking for Decru?" the Stone asked into her mind.

Shalt always seemed to know what she was thinking. She wouldn't accuse it of eavesdropping now. She was open to it. "Yes. I'm not sure if I can walk to his chambers from here."

Decru called to her, "I can draw you to me. It'd be easier. But if you wish to walk, I can show you the way."

They must have sensed her presence from the moment she drew near. No, probably since the instant her feet decided she'd angle in this direction. She thought a moment. "I have time to walk."

A series of dots appeared on the hardpacked floor of the cave, outlining the edge of the massive hole and running into the dark. She'd thought about what it might be like to explore the ways behind the stone, where Krid had been kept in a cell, where passages led to Zamani's fine rooms, and Decru's. If their quarters were ancient and fascinating, what might be on the stairs and in the hallways that led to them. How far back did they go?

She started along the line of tiny lights that grew ahead

of her. Having sight that pierced through walls did not always mean penetrating darkness. For that, she needed Vatu who'd grown up in dark underwater grottos and deep-sea ravines. So far, her vision lacked the specialized pathways that would allow neural rods to connect to circuits in her brain. When in *lanten*, she had that skill. Vatu had that or bioluminescence sensitivity at hand any time. Yanda could watch it in the amazing Mingal's eyes.

Suddenly lonely, she mind-called, "Vatu, do you want to explore with me?"

The small Mingal female appeared in front of her. "I've always wanted to see more down here."

"I thought maybe you've been missing caves." Yanda wrapped an arm around her friend's slight shoulders and started again along the light trail.

"Oo, who's showing you the way?" Vatu asked. "I'd like that skill."

Decru said into their minds, "I learned it from mushrooms. You take your mind under and send up tiny rows of lights like a mycelium thread."

Vatu's eyes glowed brighter with excitement.

Yanda created a float globe to see her friend better. As expected, the Mingal's head nubs stood on end, pulsing cerulean. "I'm sure Decru will help you practice," she said.

"Are you visiting him to learn something?" Vatu asked.

"I don't know. Maybe."

Decru responded, "You're welcome, for whatever purpose. I'm happy to have visitors. Particularly ones as multifaceted as you two."

Yanda and Vatu grinned. They breathed in the mysterious, dank, dark earth smell of millennial age that filled the caves. Holding hands, they climbed steep, narrow, curving stone steps. Arm-in-arm they walked along roughly carved out passages. The line of lights led them to a carved door and stopped.

"Enter," Decru called.

Yanda turned a handle and pushed the heavy door inward.

Decru sat at an immense desk, polished and vibrant with age as though it lived and breathed, deep funnels and sinews on its sides radiating honey-gold to deep-red, deepening to ebony. "Will you join me?" The old elf gestured to seats of molded leather that also conveyed an ancient history.

Yanda and Vatu approached and sank into the malleable cushioned chairs, taking in the scent of rich textures like old fine vintage wine that drifted up as they wiggled into comfort.

Decru lifted a hand as weathered and aged as his desk, and a tray, filled with steaming cups and fresh baked tarts that wafted sweet spices, floated in through a doorway. When it came to rest on the surface of his workspace, Decru graciously served them, sending the plates into their hands. A small table appeared between them.

Vatu giggled, her blue hand covering her delicate, sensitive mouth, which always captivated Yanda with its play of emotions.

"My hosting amuses you?" Decru was not offended. He seemed only more delighted.

Vatu let out a breath, dropping her hand to the plate she now held in her lap. "This is just so fun. It's like a magic show and…" She breathed in the room that seemed to wrap around the natural mountain shapes, with curves and dips in walls and ceiling. "Everything in here is new and yet familiar. We have mountain chambers like this in my world, but...not the same." Her lids dropped slightly to take in more than the surface. "I sense the ground. Don't you, too?" She sat up straighter, looked up and to her left. "A small rivulet, there, above. A newborn amphibian, very yellow." She turned to Yanda. "I don't see through like you. I see life, I think. Maybe I see it in other minds."

"Fabulous," Decru said with an outward breath like a sigh. "I'm so glad you came." He pondered his hands. "I was sorting." Before him on the broad desk, a number of trays held an array of items.

"I didn't see those when we arrived." Yanda had reason to be surprised. Her ability to notice details was one of the reasons she made such a fine surgeon.

"I hid them at first." Decru bowed his head as though in apology.

"Did we interrupt something private?" Yanda asked, averting her eyes rather than to try to examine his treasures.

"Oh no. Not exactly that."

Yanda sipped the milky concoction, slightly earthy in flavor, and chocolatey. "Mm." She set it on the table.

"Do you like it? It's a rendition of *kaffe*, my own brew."

Vatu tried it. "Yes. It reminds me of something. Dirt." She peeled laughter again, almost spilling her drink before she set it down. "I mean, good dirt. Like roasted ground *shapit*." She bit into a tart and smacked her lips, then took another bigger bite and brushed away crumbs.

Decru ran a hand over one tray, then another. He glanced at them, then back at his hands, touching one object after another. "Sometimes I walk very far to find these."

He picked up a stone, rubbed it, set it down, picked up wood shaped by the sea. He looked at Yanda. "I think you are troubled, by half-truths, lies, and deceptions."

"Yes, I am. At least half-truths. Lies and deceptions would indicate malice. Do you think there's that too?" she asked, then nibbled on a pastry.

"Not malice. Not by anyone close to you. I imagine they're in an effort to protect you, and also to stay safe themselves."

Yanda leaned forward. "You know things, then."

"Know," he repeated. "That is such a finite-seeming word." He picked up what looked like a crystalized coral flower and gently stroked fingertips along its edges.

Over their heads, several globe-lights floated. More illuminated the extremities of the room which seemed to lead into deep furrows, maybe more hallways.

Decru sat up taller and swept his arms over all the trays. "I like to sort, to keep certain types of energy and power at hand for times when we search for what is hidden, seek understanding in what is obscure or fleeting or evanescent." He wheezed a breath that seemed labored. "I'm having trouble deciding... Vatu—" he held out a leathery hand— "I think you might serve as oracle. There is such truth in you. Would you come around to my side and give me your hand?"

Turmoil rumbled in Yanda with this. Jealousy? Protectiveness? A sensation of being left out. Not belonging. Not good enough? All tumbled through her as her friend, unhesitating, stood and walked around the desk, her pantsuit seeming to have grown thicker and fluffier the deeper they came into the caves.

"I would hold your hand as well, Yandawi," he assured

her, "but for this, I believe touching you might only confuse me."

He held her gaze in his, dark ebony-amber eyes sending a sensation through her.

What was he conveying?

Her abdomen shivered with heat. She dropped her eyes, embarrassed. Was there something between them? What a canny old man he was, handsome, ageless, with his white and silver hair tied back, clean shaven, with walnut skin taut over fine cheekbones.

Vatu extended her delicate blue hand to him and he took it.

"Now…with me." He reached, moving the trays.

She held up her other hand, imitating his motions. Her lids lowered over cat-like eyes. After a moment, she gasped, and her hand dropped to a shiny black object with many points and markings.

"Careful." He took the obsidian from her, spoke unfamiliar words, then carefully put her hand back on it. Again, he spoke words unknown to Yanda. *"Leshkreet cantu saban."* Then he abruptly stood. Carrying the powerful stone, he moved away from the desk. "I believe we need water. Come."

He led the way into one of the alcoves which did indeed become a short passage, weaving its way further into the mountain.

Yanda knew somehow they were beneath Vashal, the power-imbued crystal mountain, now. She heard water burbling and rushing. The air grew warm. They stepped into a small grotto with a churning pool at the center, seats carved into the edges.

A hot tub, Yanda thought, and with an inner smirk. Was

he just wanting to sit naked with two females? But that could not be all. They sank to their chins in the mysterious heated waters.

Tenali appeared in the doorway.

"Join us." Decru waved him in.

The broody half-elf hesitated, then stepped into the rock grotto, shadow elongated by float globes.

Tenali dropped his clothes.

Yanda had never seen him naked. He had a fine physique. And scars she caught sight of before he slid in between her and Vatu, where they'd made space.

She couldn't help a shiver of excitement as his limbs slipped along hers.

But Decru drew her attention when he set the black obsidian on a dish floating in place at the center of the pool as if anchored. The pointy lump broadened, then flattened into a melted smooth mound. Bubbles formed inside it. Was it responding to the heat of the pool?

"Yanda, touch the *mobri*," Decru invited.

Assuming he meant the newly transformed talisman, she tentatively pressed a palm on the now malleable substance. It remained black but with other tones showing in the bubbled areas: midnight blue, turquoise, and lemon yellow. A green shade edged in. She thought of the semi-sticky ground of the Jejod's mountain. Was it the same? Did it have special properties that could tell truths?

"What do you most want to know?" Decru asked.

Yanda's foot struck Tenali's and slid away, but his came back to meet hers. Tingles spread up her leg.

Determined to focus on her hand and the power object, she shifted on the stone seat.

"Do I distract you?" Tenali asked into her mind.

Yanda glanced at Vatu and Decru. She felt their feet joining at the center of the pool. Smiles grew.

She took a deep breath. "There's not just one thing I want to know. It's a tangle. The Stones want me to bring their missing sister moon to Terlond. My parents seem to be on that moon. They deserted me as a newborn baby, I think. Who are my parents? Am I really seeing them, hearing them?" And worst of all… she didn't want to say it. Had they known all along of the abductions and Seiti's forced training on Blaz? Were they tied in somehow? "You see, people make cryptic remarks. Shouma told me she was supposed to do something to my parents, betray them or… Were her people the reason they've had to hide? They said they had to go where they didn't want me to grow up. It's all troubling…" Her voice trailed off.

Tenali touched her cheek. She hadn't realized tears rolled there. Vatu wiggled a foot against hers. Sorrowful, Decru's mahogany-gold eyes rested on her face.

The black substance under her hand had warmed. It seemed thoughts and sensations trickled into her mind from the bubbles. Then she was not in the pool. Her mind traveled. She sensed Shalt and Ash-don with her, the others in the pool, but she was merely a blob, too. Her spirit skirted the cloud world of Erzon, said hello to its kindred obsidian mountain, and traveled on.

Tenali had joined her in spirit; they were a melded bubble.

They came to the edge of the known universe.

"I hovered here," Tenali said.

"You told me you went beyond here, into Unknown Space," she said.

"I thought I did," he answered.

"Something controls our minds then," Yanda said. It was a question, and a statement. "I think we'll be drawn to Melcraf, that ooze in her, again now." Panic rose like piranhas in her belly anticipating the loss of everything she knew as when she'd been yanked to that river before. "I'm not ready." She grabbed her hand away, drew her knees up onto the rock shelf and pressed her head to them.

CHAPTER

9

"I had a chance and I blew it, forfeited it." Yanda coughed a derisive half-laugh as they walked along the path away from the caves. She hugged herself.

Vatu slid fingers under Yanda's arm. "Maybe you weren't prepared. It's good you *could* release yourself, could decide."

Yanda turned to her, eyes wide in amazement. "Good?" she repeated, lips numb. "I wonder. I told Decru I wanted to know."

Tenali, on her other side, said, "Vatu's right." He rested a hand on her neck. Squeezing lightly, he stopped her. "Sometimes…things are taking shape. It's like tearing open a flower bud before its ready."

"You think this is like that?" Yanda asked, mouth twitching down with emotion. "Or are you being metaphorical with something else?"

He stood still, hand dropping to his side. "We haven't talked."

"I can go on ahead," Vatu said.

Yanda was torn. Her kids and Ilan waited back at the treehouse. But she had unfinished business with Tenali. If she went to the hot springs with him now, they'd make love.

Did she want that? Of course she wanted that. On the other hand, she didn't.

They reached the bunker. She sensed Beri and Gisli along with Merne and Tlalit inside. She should talk to Tenali in a place where they would not drift into lovemaking. Maybe that was their destiny, but right now it would cloud everything.

"Yes, maybe I'll check in with the others, see if all is safe. Vatu, would you want to go to the treehouse ahead of me? I shouldn't be too long." Yanda cringed inside, at the battle going on within her, the deflection and deception, though she thought Vatu guessed a lot of the truth.

"You, Merne, and Tenali probably have a lot to talk about," Vatu said, saving her.

"Yeah, true." Yanda wanted to talk to Beri as well. He'd saved her daughter and they'd never spoken about it. Now she also had a conversation with Decru hanging over her. She'd left with hardly a word. What had he thought of her cowardice?

Vatu sauntered away, waving. Tenali and Yanda turned toward the underground bunker.

"I learned nothing. I'm so..." Her voice trailed off as they trotted down the steps.

"I believe what I said earlier."

"I thought you might be drawing a parallel with you and me. Is that why you left Alland, really? You thought our love was a rosebud not to be opened yet?"

He eased her around to look at him. "I went to find your daughter."

"Without me. Why?"

"I thought I had a lead."

"You thought you'd run off and be a hero. Like when you dropped me with Krid. You were a man on a mission, and collateral damage didn't matter."

In all the conversations she'd had with him in her head, she'd never torn into him like this. But she plunged on, "You'd collect all the Stone fragments yourself, save your elven people, put the land back together." Who was this talking?

He stared at her, clearly wondering the same thing. "You really believe that?"

They perched against the long counter that ran the length of the first level. The room was dark but for dim strands of lights at the floor and ceiling edges.

"Of course I do. It's what you do. What lead? Tlalit and your mom came to me months later, in the outback of Alland, when they found footage of Seiti or some little girl on Shagal. I'd been through hell, been betrayed…"

He took her hand. "I'm sorry I wasn't with you for that. I thought—"

"What lead?" she asked again.

"Well, now I think it was Melcraf."

"You had a vision." Yanda kept her hand on the edge of the desk, letting his rest on hers. Her voice sounded dead to her.

"I was told by someone—maybe your parents—that they could help me bring the ship into Unknown Space, and help me find Seiti."

Yanda yanked her hand away. "So, you'd be the first

explorer there, too. You couldn't resist. What did they do? Did they help you fly to Melcraf?"

He rubbed his face. "No. They brought my spirit. I saw the same sight you saw, of your daughter dancing on the surface of a moon where no one could breathe." His voice was gravelly with emotion.

"But you still thought...what?" Yanda grew quiet.

"I hoped, stupidly, that I would bring her back to you."

"You've told your mom all this?"

"No, we haven't spoken that much either."

"Why do you do this?" Yanda stepped to him and wrapped her arms around him. "Why do you blunder out on your own?" She held him, shaking her head against his chest. She understood him. She was like him, in ways, depending only on herself. She heard footsteps and opened her eyes. Merne stood ten feet away. Tlalit, Beri, and Gisli came up next to her, studying Yanda and Tenali. Beri a quirked smile. Gisli looked down and shuffled his feet.

"We were hoping to talk with you," Merne said.

Yanda pushed away from Tenali. "We do need to talk. Is war averted?"

"For the moment," Tlalit answered, arms crossed. She shared the others' bemused expressions.

"Tenali and I were just with Decru," Yanda said. "He had a substance that sent us on a vision journey to the edge of the Known Universe and..." Yanda shrugged, glancing at Tenali. What to say? Had they seen anything worth mentioning? Yet she wanted to bring the others into the discussion.

"Yanda's wondering about the wisdom of drawing Melcraf here," Tenali said.

"Ilan's brought up concern as well," Yanda said, "about drawing the moon here."

Tenali scowled at the mention of Ilan's opinion.

Merne lifted a hand to stop Yanda. "Let's have a good natter below where it's more comfortable. I'll make tea." She led the way.

Halfway down the stairs, Yanda stopped. "Could you four talk? I'd like to have a little time with Beri. We haven't had a chance to catch up." Yanda realized that, much as being with Tenali had warmed her heart, she could use a break from the intensity of being around him.

It was sunset when she and Beri stepped out of the bunker onto the path. Rail-thin, the red-haired man grinned down at her and ruffled her hair, like he'd always done. Even when she was still captive in the Citadel and reached her mind to him, he'd ruffled her hair with his spirit hand.

She smiled up at him and took his hand. Tan and rusty freckles roughened the back of it.

"Sit on a rock?" she asked.

"Yeah, there's one with a good view past the first pools." He trotted out onto a ledge that led around the pools and past falls.

"We didn't get that much time together once we reached Rotoul." She followed, jumping from rock to rock.

"You were busy saving the Great Stone and important stuff like that." He winked back at her.

They traipsed through forest single file and came out on a cliff shelf that looked out over forest clear to the ocean.

"Ooh. I've never been here." Yanda stared toward the sea where she'd swum with dolphin-like *tesu*.

"I thought you might not have. We can sit over here."

Beri climbed to a hummock of wild grasses and, folding his long legs, made room for her.

Yanda dropped next to him and pulled a grass blade with a tuft at the end. Tapping it against her lips, she gazed into the distance. After a moment of silence, she asked, "How'd you and Gisli find each other again? I thought you were off with a lover on Sandu, and Gisli'd gone home to Tellot."

Beri crossed his legs and settled back against a large stone. "That was all true, for a while." He glanced at her, mouth pressed in a half-smile. "Your adventures are much more worth telling. I want to hear everything."

"Not true. You first. Mine requires a case of beer." She gave him one of her no-nonsense stares.

He looked down at leaves he was splintering in his hands. "I went to Alland."

She sat up. "You what?"

"It's true. I was worried about you. I also had information, related not just to you but about—"

"Why did you never contact me? Don't tell me. You were after a power object." All Beri's troubles came from seeking objects of power, sometimes for noble reasons, such as to capture the *sophis tetra* back from Krid. Which had caused him a couple of years of indentured servitude.

"Maybe, but also Tellot. That *wagensi* who betrayed you? In the Sinisay? She's a piece of work. And Ilan was on the trail of...we were crossing paths in some of our—"

"You and Ilan?" Yanda said. Suspicion wiggled its way into her mind.

"And Gisli. When you went back to your planet and Ilan found Tregen, Merne jumped into her head. I knew then, too, everything they learned."

"Tregen? Who's this Tregen? And what were you doing in Ilan's mind?"

"They never told you her name? The one who sold out you and your daughter out? She and Krid do deals. I was telling you, Ilan and Gisli were searching using *MNN*. Some of their threads overlapped, were leading us to the same sources." Beri twisted his hands together, then picked at a callus, examining it carefully.

Yanda realized once again, Ilan had kept things from her. "Why didn't Ilan tell me?"

"Maybe to keep you safe. Right then, we knew about Blaz and Tiklet, and...we went."

"You went. You just walked onto Blaz, no problem?"

"No, it was a problem. See...Prok..."

At the mention, Yanda remembered Ilan wanting to take her to a library on of Prokit's Moon.

"...Tlalit had told Gisli a lot about Prok," Beri went on, "how you can go into those rooms, completely encrypted, and walk highways and byways, finding out what's hidden."

"We were there. We should have...I could have saved Seiti sooner."

Beri gripped Yanda's shoulder. "I want to take them all down."

"Ow!" She winced.

But he was on a roll. "We have to do more. We saved Seiti but there are others there. People like Tregen and Krid selling them out." He was breathing hard, like a bull working up to charge. "Places like Tellot will be gone. We let them keep exploiting the weaker worlds. We let those with power, sinister aims for power, on Blaz, and Qontaq! Torturing those with abilities they want. Do you think the

Jejods will have their world? No. Not with Tiklet training weapons. Innocent kids no one suspects."

Yanda asked, "Are you writing articles about all this?"

"Not yet. There's more to do. I have to interview Decru. He knows a lot. He's been alive forever. Can you get me an audience with him?"

Yanda scrambled to her feet. "Slow down, journal-man. I love what you're saying, and I'm with you one-hun-dred-percent. But you…" She turned to walk back as the sun set over the mountains and shadows grew, "but just ease off, okay? Have a care." She turned back and reached a hand to him.

He pulled to standing, not really using her for more than ballast.

"Thank you, for saving Seiti." She stared up at him, tears in her eyes. "I have to tell Gisli, too." She swallowed a lump.

He bent and kissed her lips. "You're welcome." He strode away past her.

On Farn and Terlond, as fellow captives, she'd found Beri kind, a good friend. She'd known he could be reckless. He'd never kissed her on the mouth before. Had he changed? What had come over him? She had to admit she'd wondered if he was attracted to her. He was her friend, her first friend when she'd been abducted and imprisoned. She'd valued that so much at the time. And now it had been so long since they'd spent any time together.

She left the kiss hanging in the air, letting it be what he said it was, merely a way of showing thanks, not wanting to confront any more complicated feelings.

She followed, sensing a tap in her mind. Ilan was checking on her. "I'm okay. Talking with Beri. Catching up," she said to Ilan in mind-speak, hiding thoughts for now of what she'd learned from Beri, things he should have told her sooner. She needed to plan before confronting him. As they rounded the last outcropping, she heard elven singing. "It must be dinner," she said.

"Yeah. we can cut through here."

They turned on a well-worn path before reaching the bunker, and soon came out into the glade where elven lights were strung through the trees. Delicious smells wafted from the long tables. The elves stood, sending up sounds of harmonies as Yanda and Beri slipped to empty seats. A little way down the table, Zami stood on a bench next to Zamani, singing with the rest. He could pick up the words from their minds as though the tunes were in his cells. He waved to her as the song came to an end and all sat.

Yanda realized she'd only had scones with Decru in the last several hours. Her stomach growled as she helped herself to sauteed mushrooms in thick sauce, and dolloped it over a mound of grain on her plate. There were more empty seats around them. Merne, spotting her, came to sit across from them. Tenali and Gisli joined them as well. She had a feeling a meeting was coming on.

Tenali gave her a look. "You deserted me," he said in mind-speak.

"Beri and I had a lot of catching up to do." She thought about all she'd learned, long overdue.

Far down the next table, she spotted Ilan's tall form topped with red-gold hair. Next to him sat Seiti and Vatu. Yanda wished she were with them. She never felt she could get enough time with her daughter, after two years away from her. But then she glanced at Beri next to her. And

Tenali across the table. She had a wealth of reunions to appreciate.

CHAPTER

10

Z amani stood. "Tomorrow we will have a council of both the Circles."

"I want you in the water here," Ash-don said into Yanda's mind.

"No. You should be with me, on my surface," Shalt countered.

Yanda shifted, uncomfortable with the tension around where she should be. She spoke with the Stones alone, by mind-speak, "Wherever I am, I need to know everything about Melcraf. I need to know the truth. Are my parents on that moon? Is Melcraf dangerous? You've hinted that she can 'take care of herself'. Maybe I should go to where you two meet." She had thought about that place, the feeling of slipping in *lanten* to the crevice between the great stones, or moons, deep in the sea.

"Can you keep your intellectual faculties when in that sea creature state?" Shalt asked. "Perhaps it is best for you to be with Decru for facing Melcraf's...pet."

Yanda perceived then that Decru sat at the next table, eyes on her. He didn't often join them for the large communal meals, finding it overstimulating, she surmised. "You're here," she said into his mind as their eyes met.

"I can come into the sea with you," Decru responded.

Sensing the conversation between Yanda, the Stones, and Decru, Zamani stopped speaking. He had to defer to Decru, his elder, and bowed toward him.

Yanda discerned strong feeling between the two male elves and had second thoughts but the two seemed to have decided she would go with Decru to the crevice between the Stones.

"So be it. Dusk tomorrow." Zamani sat.

"What was that?" Beri asked. "Is that Decru?"

"Leave him alone." Yanda scooped a bite of mushroom paté with flat bread.

"His energy is palpable, isn't it?" Beri was clearly fascinated.

She put a hand on Beri's arm, across the table. "Can you wait until I know more? What is it you want to ask him, anyway?"

"The history of everything here," Beri said, sitting forward with lively eyes on her. "How long the elves have been here and if they were elsewhere before. About that golden city in the tunnels outside of Dondar."

She'd heard Xentu built it. Was it true? "I'd like those answers, too." She worked on her diminishing pile of savory grains and sauces, forest root vegetables, and artisan breads.

"Then we should go to him together."

"Well, we have this thing tomorrow."

"After tomorrow." Beri's eyes blazed with eagerness.

Decru stood, his body straight as a young sapling though he moved slowly. "You must come to me early. We have much to prepare," he conveyed into Yanda's mind. He walked away, his carved staff thumping with each step.

Plates were cleared and desserts served.

Yanda stood. "If you'll excuse me," she said to her friends sitting around her. They nodded with understanding as she took her dessert with her to the next table.

Seeing her approach, Vatu made room on the bench between her and Seiti. As soon as Yanda had settled, Zami hurried to her and she swept him into her lap, kissing his cheeks. Between smooches, she said, "I missed you."

"Why were you gone so long?" he asked, picking up a cake crumble and popping it in his mouth.

"So many old friends. Beri's here. You should tell him how you've kept the little elephant he made you." She forked a bite of dessert and nudged Vatu. "Thank you."

"You know it's my pleasure." Vatu shook her heads. Nubs wobbled. "Where else would I be?"

Ilan watched Yanda.

"Thanks," she mouthed to him, too. Then she took Seiti's hand. "What have you been up to today?"

Seiti looked serious. "Ilan and I researched devices for me. He's going to teach me—"

"And she's going to teach *me*," Ilan said, holding Yanda's gaze an extra meaningful second.

Yanda knew he meant he'd find out what they'd been teaching her at Tiklet and was grateful.

"Tlalit says we can get it in Dondar, no problem," Seiti said, shifting on the bench in her excitement. "There are even tech outlets on the edge of Sheffed supplied straight off ships."

"I can imagine," Ilan said, chewing a golden layered brownie.

"You mean contraband?" Yanda asked in mind-speak just for him. "And Sheffed seemed so sweet."

Tlalit and Merne seemed to catch their thoughts.

Tlalit laughed. "The things we could tell you."

"I wish you would," Yanda thought into the small mind-meld. Subtext underlaid her remark.

"I want this silvery blue one," Seiti was saying. "It's lightweight. Of course, you can make it all holographic." She put her hands together as if holding a small ball. "But there are things you want physical plaz and circuits for." She looked up at her mother, brows raised. "You know?"

"I do know, squash blossom." Yanda pulled her daughter into a squeeze.

Seiti's eyes teared up. "I remember you calling me that. I whispered it to myself to feel you near me."

Zami wiggled around and hugged his sister, sensing her emotion.

She grinned at her little brother. "You have cake on your cheek, silly." She brushed off a patch of honey and crumbs.

"How about hot *chaka* in the treehouse, with jammies on?" Yanda suggested.

Ilan nodded. "Great idea."

An hour later, Zami climbed into Yanda's bunk. It was more a split-level, extending out into a tree bole with space around the sides of the bed for shelves and tables. She had started making the area hers, with the few favorite objects she'd kept through her travels. Yanda patted beside her and Zami climbed in under the covers. They snuggled and read a book while, below, Ilan and Seiti explored on his ENAC that was twice as powerful as Yanda's. At the time she bought it, she thought it was state of the art. That was nearly four years before.

"Mom, when can we go to Dondar?" Seiti called up to her.

Yanda cringed at the name of the city where she'd lived in captivity. Was Shouma right, that she needed to see it again to start to heal from her experience there?

When she was silent a moment too long, Ilan said, "It seems like Sheffed's the place to go. I'll find out. Maybe after tomorrow." He paused. "Right?"

"Yes, after tomorrow. That'll be a fun excursion." Yanda's obligations for after tomorrow were mounting. Go with Beri to Decru. Shop in Sheffed. She wondered how they'd get there. She'd left Sheffed through tunnels.

After a second book, Zami's eyelids drooped. Yanda coaxed him to lie on his side and tucked the covers around him. She dimmed the float globes with her mind and snugged her arm over him. Her mind wandered to the next day. She'd spirit traveled into the sea with both Zamani and Tenali. Those had been amorous occasions, a complete meld of mind and body. What would it be like with Decru?

"I'll let you all sleep," Ilan said. Yanda heard him get up.

"Good night," Seiti said to him as he left. "'Night, Mom. And Zami."

Zami murmured a sleepy, "'Night."

"Kiss kiss," Yanda said, wondering if she should climb down and give her daughter a hug. "Want to come up with us? There's room."

"I'm going to draw for a while." Seiti slid her book out.

Yanda heard the pages turn and smiled to herself, pleased that Seiti loved art.

As Zami's breathing grew steady in sleep, Yanda lay pondering. Looking above the woven barrier, she saw stars among dense branches. A breeze stirred them, shifting the spots of light in the dark sky. The treehouse swayed slightly.

She thought about Beri's kiss. She thought about his face, the raw look in his eyes that had always drawn her. With his coppery hair, he had light eyelashes and brows. Still, there was something appealing about his look. His intelligence, and loyalty to their friendship were irresistible. He'd come to Alland to tell her what he'd found out. She'd have liked to know he was there.

Zami breathed in deep and let out a sigh in his sleep, turning to his back. She studied his perfect features, his rosebud mouth, and ached with love. It was always an ache because he'd always seemed like her stolen treasure.

She closed her eyes and tried to keep them shut.

In his bedroom, Ilan's thoughts were about her. She could tell he tried to keep them from disturbing her. She let the heat of them sift into a corner of her mind so that there was room for other thinking: Tenali, Ilan, Zamani. Now Beri seemed to have raised in temperature. And tomorrow, Decru would fill her day.

Yanda sat with Ilan, Vatu, and the kids on the veranda. Peeks of sea shone in the distance through leafy branches.

"What will you all be up to today?" she asked. She could think of little but her impending work with Decru. She wondered how early he'd meant for her to arrive, and if he'd call for her or expect her to know when to come.

Seiti brushed crumbs from the corner of her mouth. "I'd like to see the gym. Tlalit said there's good exercise equipment, all I could want. I feel like a slug."

"That sounds good. The exercise room is on a lower level of the bunker, where the elves have had to live for periods of time when under siege by colonists." Yanda finished her last gulp of *kaffe*, popped a remaining bite of morning bun into her mouth, and took her dishes to the kitchen. "Shall we head to the bunker?"

As Seiti carried her dish to the kitchen, Yanda noticed her daughter's straight-backed, gliding stride. This was nothing like the young girl who'd romped and twirled, dancing and flopping onto furniture. Her posture and way of moving had to come from highly trained muscles.

Seiti said Tiklet staff tested their limits after sports. What was the extent of the training?

Yanda shivered as this latest evidence of weaponizing children took shape before her. "I've seen the long room with climbing ropes and *plubber* balls but haven't used it." Yanda took Seiti's dish and rinsed it.

Collecting backpacks and other sundry items, the five descended to the forest path.

Yanda thought the excursion would help take her mind off Decru but it didn't. As she ambled between her kids, questions swirled in her mind. What kind of preparation did he think she needed? She'd gone to the ocean depths before. Did he want to train her to keep her full faculties while in *lanten* state?

She remembered the first time Decru took her hand; a painful energy had surged through her. She'd been changed by it. Would it be like that? Yanda chewed a fingernail, fear building.

Zami took her hand, reminding her to be present with her family.

"Hey Button, we're going to work out. High bars for you to fly to!" She smiled at him and squeezed his hand.

He grinned up and skipped.

Arriving at the bunker, they filed to the third underground level. Instead of banks of screens, they arrived in a comfortable sitting area with couches and thick rugs. Clear plaz panels looked onto a garden with vine-covered walls, as they walked the length of a room. Light filtered three levels underground by means of cleverly embedded reflective surfaces.

A sliding panel gave onto the next corridor where Tlalit and Merne joined them. The last section opened onto a spacious gym. Skylights strategically accessed from levels above sent rays of natural light around the room. Some had rainbow colors.

The room was not empty. Beri and Gisli pumped weights. Beri stood with a wide grin when he saw her. She called "good morning" and he came over. They hugged. She caught his thought. He knew she was going to Decru and clearly wanted to be invited. "Sorry. Not this time," she thought into his mind and patted his arm.

As with all elven undergrounds and caves, fresh air circulated.

Seiti strode to a rope structure and swung up with ease from rope-to-rope. grabbing a bar and flipping to land on her feet on a platform high above. "It's tempting to use floating like Zami's shown me," Seiti called down, "but I want to resist and use my own strength."

She sounds so much older than she is. Not like an eight-year-old, Yanda thought. I need to get her around kids. She made a mental note to find out what elf children were a similar age.

Zami spotted Tik perched on one of the high bars, nearly in shadow at a corner of the ceiling. He flew to her, pumping invisible wings. Yanda's heart lurched, as it always did when he reached those heights, suspended in air.

Decru's voice sounded in Yanda's head. "I see you're close by. Are you ready to come to me?"

Yanda glanced from Seiti to Zami. But her kids were in a good place, busy, occupied, with watchful guardians.

Ilan had joined the men at the weights. Vatu climbed a knotty rope in sinewy movements.

Yanda said, "I'm summoned to my training with Decru. I'll…" She had no idea how long she'd be or what she'd encounter. "I'll be in touch…soon-ish." She sent a mental kiss to each of her kids and turned to leave.

Outside the door, she said to Decru, "Want to bring me?"

CHAPTER

11

Yanda stood in Decru's main chamber. Reticent about his preparation, she was nevertheless excited for it as she looked around. He was nowhere in sight.

"Refreshments?" Decru stood across the room in one of the deep dark alcoves, statuesque, with his walnut skin and smooth, defined features. Had he been there, invisible, or had he just appeared?

"We've had *kaffe* and buns," Yanda said. "But thank you."

"We're going to use a lot of inner resources. Drink this." A tall fluted receptacle filled with bright orange liquid floated toward her. Putting up her hand, she received it and drank. Fruity, also astringent, it sent a charge down through her. She noted a change in perception. Her chest heaved with fast breaths as she adjusted.

He took her hand. How had he gotten to her so swiftly?

Her thoughts scattered.

He took her shoulders and gazed into her eyes. "Discipline." His voice pounded like an echo chamber in her head. He pushed her glass to her.

She was sure she'd emptied it but now it was filled with crystalline water. She drank again. It helped to clear her mind.

"All life is full and empty. All time is now and forever."

She wouldn't remember all his lessons in the days and years that followed. But his words created an atmosphere in her head that helped her take in experiences in the moment.

Yanda and Decru sank, naked, in warm water. The water cooled. She didn't care; she was *lanten* now. So was he. His sea-creature eyes took in hers. She took in his. They were one, blended. Their seal-like skin touched, sweet and electrifying as they left ice-cold sea caves and subterranean rivers to shoot out into open waters. They flipped and twirled.

Tesu joined them, and they swam distances, arcing out of the water, soaring in long leaps.

Then it was as though they sat in a room. Decru gripped her shoulders again. "You are *lanten* and you are Xentu." This time it was not gentle. It ached and...

Did they make love?

No, they were in all states: walking, climbing, caressing, lying still.

"Purge the wild so you can feel it trickle back in," he coached her. "Control it."

Was he facing her? Holding her from behind?

"It's only us here. Banish others from your thoughts," he prompted.

She felt suddenly alone. Love and affection drained from her. But then she sourced a deep well of emotion that was eternal and primal, clear of complications, worries, challenges that wracked her every day.

"Yes, that's where it is," Decru said softly. "You need to find a way to draw on it, every time. Each moment that you go wild, you must also resource your greatest inner knowing." He stroked her back.

Or her front. He was everywhere, in her and around her.

They did make love, and they didn't. It didn't matter. It was a memory and an illusion.

Deep in the sea, they sank through dark waters toward the crevice of the Great Stones.

"Do you feel strong? Can you draw on that place at will?" he asked her. "Even when you face the black smoke serpent?"

"Maybe I need more practice." In her full faculties, yet also *lanten*, she battled uncertainty.

"I think not."

He was with her as they sank; they were one, then they were separate. Again, they were one, then separate. She took in the sea through her gills and noticed its nourishing elements. She longed to return to the *tesu*, to explore sea caves and abandon the plan of finding everything out at last.

How long had they been in the water? It seemed like years. She slid into Decru's arms and they kissed, languidly. Then he was gone. No, he was part of her.

Then they were at the crevice, sliding between the two moons, melding into the great stones, sensing the powerful circles of the Neyna and Neyla elves. The energies of the massive mind-meld filled her. For a moment, they pinned her in overwhelming sensation. Then she washed it all out, and let it trickle in again, controlled, as she'd learned.

Her parents joined, permeating the meld with a troubling tone. Even sinister, Yanda thought, hugging herself with spirit arms, for of course they were in spirit form within the Stones.

She wanted answers, had to have them. After all, she was central to this decision. Apparently the moons needed her skills to pull Melcraf to them. But every time Dal'an and Ebri appeared, purportedly on the surface of a moon in Unknown Space where no one could sustain life, she had to wonder if it was a deception.

Disembodied inside the stones, deep under the sea, Yanda slowly turned to Decru and let herself slip into his mind, in the way she had gone into Ilan's once to save Bonden. "I want you to face Grethon, not me. You ask the questions, and perceive if my parents are really on Melcraf. Assess if it's safe to bring the sister moon here."

"We're with the Circles. All will speak to them. All will assess," Decru answered.

Yanda detected puzzlement as she floated in spirit, inside Decru and in the Stones.

"This time I want to be enfolded in your mind, not in mine. Are you willing?" she asked from her heart, more vulnerable than she normally let herself be. "I want to think and feel as you, and through you for this."

She felt herself an infant and then a child, as though she observed another's life. She realized Decru accessed her oldest memories.

"Why didn't we do this before?" she asked him. "I could have found answers about my parents."

"But you understood only as a baby and as a toddler," he said. "We can retrieve only so much."

"Why do you show this to me now?" she asked.

"So you realize that then is now, and now is then. Time is relative. You were strong then and you are stronger now."

"Can we confirm where my parents are, and what they want?" Yanda asked.

She tired of philosophy and perspective. This was her chance. And she needed to get it behind her. Then she could focus on bringing Seiti back to well-being, detecting and removing anything Tiklet might have been inserted into her that might grow inside her and twist her life. Or put all of them in danger. Then she, Beri, Ilan and the rest had bigger challenges to tackle, so that no child would be weaponized again.

Were her parents' part of a solution, or a new problem?

Had they ever been in league with the Sinisay and other power vampires?

"Yes. Of course. We must know." Decru had arrived in the adult years of her memory and now his spirit held hers fully. "We are ready," he announced to all the mind-meld waiting for them.

It had only taken seconds but seemed like light years.

This time when Yanda saw her parents in a smoky chamber, clarity grew. As in the Jejods' cloud world, her mind seemed to calibrate and remove obscurity. Dal'an and Ebri stood before her, sharp features stark and clear. She gasped at the severity and force in them.

"Are you sure you don't want to ask them questions directly?" Decru said to her.

"I'll ask you and you speak," she said firmly.

In spirit form, they could choose to appear standing

before the Xentu couple in the caves of Melcraf. As speaker, Decru let himself be seen.

"Very well," he said to her, then asked for all the mind-meld to hear, "Yanda would like to know if you are in fact upon Melcraf in Unknown Space."

Dal'an's eyes widened. "Decru, it has been long and long."

"It has," he responded, expression austere, giving away nothing. "Will you answer her question completely and with candor?"

"Why does Yanda not appear before us?" her mother asked, face pinched in disapproval.

"She does not wish to at this time. Will you answer?"

Yanda hugged Decru for his willingness to do as she asked.

"A form of us is on Melcraf, and Melcraf is in Unknown Space." Ebri spoke this time, cryptically.

"I assume you have only one material body. Is that on Melcraf?" Decru specified.

Dal'an folded her long hands in front of her. "For this moment, yes."

"How can that be, without oxygen. Is it the smoke that sustains you?" Decru asked.

Decru then suddenly stood with Da'lan and Ebri on the bridge over the roiling black river of smoke.

A being rose, shiny and black. Man or woman, it was impossible to say. Its mouth opened like a black hole beneath hollow eye sockets, and a sound emerged, shrill, whining, and sweet all at once, hitting multiple notes simultaneously like a stringed instrument.

"I make life possible where no life can be," Grethon sang.

Yanda shivered at the arrogance.

Dal'an brushed her hands down the fabric of her narrow,

straight gown. "But we have other places. The Golden City on Terlond. Sometimes Alland. And the Sonda have invited us to Elznap several times."

"Who is after you?" Yanda asked, accidentally posing the question directly.

"This is not important," Ebri said, eyes flinty, searching for her in the space around Decru.

"Of course it is," Decru countered, "if we are to decide whether Yanda will help pull Melcraf here."

Dal'an tried to form a personal connection to Yanda's mind but Decru prevented it, respecting her wish to be impervious.

"I shouldn't have spoken with my own voice," she whispered into Decru's mind, shrinking at her father's fierce stare.

"You'll have to learn to face them," he said kindly.

"As you said, I've had no training. They're strangers to me." She said this only to Decru.

"Why do you want Melcraf brought into orbit around Terlond?" Decru asked the Xentu parents. "Do you wish to terraform it and make a home for the Xentu people?"

"It is not we who have asked this. Once Shalt and Ashdon discovered their sister moon, they wanted to bring her back into orbit with them, as they were for millions of years." Ebri took out what seemed to be a pipe and put it to his lips.

"Why are you on Melcraf?" Decru pursued.

"We had to hide." Dal'an offered no further explanation.

"From whom? And why did you desert your daughter?" Decru asked.

The question had troubled Yanda most of her life but she winced to hear it voiced to her parents.

"We hoped to spare her this life. We left guardians," Dal'an defended.

"Guardians who taught her nothing of who she is, of her powers or how to manage them. In fact, they vilified them," Decru scolded.

The elves in the two circles, and the Stones, listened. Yanda thought she detected anger among them.

"You know nothing of it," Dal'an snapped, voice like ice. "You have your elven clans. And the great stones to care for you."

Shalt rumbled. Disturbed vibrations ran through the two stones.

"Melcraf does not provide similar care?" Decru asked.

"How can she? Alone out here in hostile dark matter? She cannot evolve." Fear crept into Dal'an's eyes as her mouth snapped shut as if she would say no more.

Seeing this, the Stones and elven circles closed out the Xentu, Melcraf, and Grethon so that they could discuss the matter without them.

Decru and Yanda were again within the Great Stones back on Terlond, no longer seeing the black smoke river that was Grethon, or Yanda's severe, imposing Xentu parents.

Yanda relaxed to be away from them. "Is it the black smoke serpent she fears?"

"I believe so," Ash-don said. "Another reason to have them closer."

"Is it, though?" Yanda had wondered if the smoke was what they'd pulled from Bonden, which made her suspect her parents might be involved with the Qontaqis who captured and tortured Bonden. Maybe they'd used the black smoke to make deals for their safety. She had no idea what their ethics were but she'd never perceived warmth in them.

"The Stones want it. It would be hard to refuse them," Decru said to her. "This conversation will help us know the whole picture."

"Yes. True. But this must seem so small and insignificant to them compared to millions of years of orbiting together." She asked Shalt and Ash-don, "Was there a special hive-mind among you when you three orbited together?"

"We used to all three orbit a planet in Known Space. Something pulled her away and sent us here as Terlond was forming," Shalt explained, "and we two became embedded. We imagine Melcraf can be put into orbit around Terlond, since she cannot be shoved into the planet." The Stone shivered in that way that meant Shalt chuckled from his own humor.

"I remember that last part but you never spoke of her."

"We'd nearly forgotten her," Shalt said.

"That's not true," Ash-don argued. "We thought she might have been obliterated, collided with another space object, when we no longer sensed her."

"You must be very excited to know she's still intact, and anxious to have that...synergy," Yanda offered.

"We are...excited." The Great Stone seemed to taste the word, exploring the emotions it might depict. "Have you learned enough?"

"Not yet, but it's a lot to mull over," Yanda said. In truth she was overloaded by contact with her frightening parents.

Into Yanda's mind only, Decru said, "I have ideas. I agree that we should end this meeting. I have some directions of inquiry to pursue."

Yanda caught a vague, anxious thought from Ilan's mind, "I need to show you something." How had he penetrated the mind-meld? But there was little Ilan could not do. Heck, he might have followed every experience of her past hours. She hoped not.

CHAPTER

12

Yanda had climbed the side of Vashal, bone-weary and hollowed out, as though she'd come out of a drug trip or prolonged illness. Sitting alone, with dry grass pricking her skin, she breathed in wild herbs' pungent scents, and stared at the distant sea.

Del'an and Ebri had answered the question of where they were, to some degree. They said they could survive in unknown space with the help of Grethon's smoke. Or did Grethon say that? Yet she still did not know who threatened them, enough to make them desert her and hide on Melcraf which had to surely be a limited existence. Del'an appeared frightened after she said that Melcraf could not evolve there.

Was Grethon controlling them? Had the creature, or entity, drawn Melcraf there to exist on? Drawn the Xentu?

How could she obtain the answers to these questions that still remained? She hugged her knees and rocked. With her mind inside Decru's, her parents —or was it Grethon?—

had not pulled her, alone, to that cavern on Melcraf. She'd heard the questions and answers along with the elves and the Stones but had not been vulnerable. Decru had surrounded her, bringing warmth, companionship, not the abandonment she'd felt when they pulled her to them before.

She rested her chin on a knee and brought back the sensation of oneness, the beautiful time with the *tesu*, the love.

She needed to go to Ilan and find out what he'd learned, but she'd spend a little more time by herself, in the late afternoon sunshine. She plucked a leaf and crushed it, pressed it to her nose and breathed in its pungent fragrance.

Did it make sense to draw Grethon to the Known Universe? Did she want to be responsible for that? How did the Qontaqis get hold of that smoke?

It *was* time to talk to Ilan. She stood, and only then, saw his large figure climbing up the hill toward her, device folded under one arm. The sun cast orange light on him from a violet sky. He drew closer. Sweat beaded his brow. He brushed it away and wiped his hand on cargo shorts.

"Did you have a good time in the gym?" she asked.

"Oh yeah," he said, slightly out of breath. He dropped to the ground and she sat near him. "We stayed maybe another half hour, then went up to the data area. Seiti has quite a scope of knowledge in those environments. And Zami. You should see him with Tlalit. Those two get crazy with cyber rooms. Of course, Merne dropped into explorations with Gisli and Beri. They want Chin—" He paused. "You probably have a lot to share."

"I caught your voice at the end. Did you join the meld

for much of it?" she asked, hands pressed to the dry ground behind her.

He perused her face, as though reluctant to be honest. "You know your mind is...well, you've been in my mind so we've made a pretty deep groove there. It's like AI. Channels get set and then they're ready to receive similar signals."

"Are you saying you heard a lot of what I heard?" she asked, a grin hovering. "What about my...training with Decru."

"That was pretty heady stuff," he said, his old confident demeanor reinserting itself. "But he was keeping the details hidden." He glanced down, then up again to her. "You were, too," he hastened to add.

"Oh, was I?" she asked. She didn't mind if he knew it all, she realized. She wanted to trust Ilan. She believed in his loyalty. She had to believe in someone's, and there was no better ally than Ilan.

"I think you were." He turned crossed legs toward her and rested his chin on folded hands. "I suspectiogpo, you learned a lot."

"What gives you that idea?" she asked, voice playful.

"You're giving off something, a vibe. It's...kind of...forceful."

"Really?"

He took her hands. "Yeah, I sense it."

She pulled her hands away, glancing at the device he'd set down next to him. "What did you want to show me? It sounded important." Seeing hurt in his eyes, she grabbed his fingers, then got on her knees and hugged him. His bulk reassured her. She breathed in a shuddering breath, and let her cheek rest on his shoulder. He pulled her onto his lap and wrapped his arms around her. They stayed that way for long minutes, then he said into her ear, "I've found a lead regarding Grethon and the black smoke."

She slid off his lap and knelt. She rubbed the back of a dusty hand across unshed tears, oblivious to the grime.

"Maybe we should go to the bunker. You can wash your hands and we can put up more screens." He stood and offered her a lift up.

As they trundled down the hill, he explained more. "Tlalit turned me on to a Prokit room. It's like a den with a thousand burrows waiting to be jumped down. Questions like who's behind what can reveal answers."

"How do they break open what must be incredibly protected?" she asked.

They held hands. Yanda hardly noticed. When she did, she almost pulled away but didn't. He kept hold of her hand as they came to the forest path and soon approached the bunker. At the stairs down, he went ahead, eagerly taking steps two at a time to the second level. That was Tlalit and Merne's favorite area, and now it was Gisli and Beri's favorite as well.

Seeing them all there, Yanda held back. "I should go see my kids."

"They're on Level 3 with Arsat and Bend," Tlalit called out. "They were getting snacks and also I think playing a chase game on the structures in the gym."

Yanda figured they'd love that but checked into their minds. First she asked Zami, "Are you having fun?"

"You're in the bunker," he said more than asked, probably sensing her on the floor above him.

"I am," she affirmed.

"You okay?" he asked.

"Yes, I spoke to your other grandparents. We're trying to figure things out."

"The scary ones?" he wondered.

She paused, surprised by that. Had he called them scary before? "I hope someday we'll know them as other than scary," she said, putting a smile into it, and a hug. "I'll see you soon. You go on playing for a bit."

"Then we swim?" he asked.

"I imagine we could, a nice sunset bathe."

"Goody."

She saw through his eyes as he soared down toward the teen elf named Bend who had arms up to catch him.

Next, she tapped into Seiti's mind. That was something she'd done less in the past two years; she made her presence known with both love and trepidation. "Hi, sweety. Are you having a nice afternoon?"

"I am, Mom. Are you back?"

She thought her daughter only asked to be polite, that she knew formidable amounts and kept track at all times. She couldn't explain how she had developed that idea. It was a sense.

"Just got here. I was training with Decru and then we had a meeting to figure out—"

"I know. Bringing Melcraf to orbit around Terlond."

"Yes, Exactly. And of course—"

"My grandparents are on Melcraf. I have more to tell you about that. A lot more."

Yanda's hands froze as she was pulling herself closer to a screen on the floor above. Her heart raced. "I always wondered if that was the case, or an illusion. Can we...can we talk about it soon?"

"Yes, I think we should," Seiti said. She seemed a tiny

bit amused but mostly far more circumspect than an eight-year-old had any right to be. "And I want to," Seiti added.

"Well, Ilan was just going to show me something important about where the Xentu are. Maybe you should be part of this. You might know more."

"I'll be right up. Should I leave Zami with Bend and Arsat?"

"Yes, that will be fine for the moment. Thank you for asking." Yanda loved how Seiti had taken to her little brother. She had never once said anything to indicate resentment that Zami had come into Yanda's life, had had access to their mother, while Seiti was away, abducted.

Seconds later, her daughter hurried toward them.

Ilan held out an unusual headset to her. "An AI hat." He quirked a miniscule smile. "It'll pick up more."

Yanda watched Seiti's expression as she received the apparatus with colorful knobs and wires. She looked haunted by the sight; Yanda feared it triggered unpleasant memories at Tiklet.

The group spent fifteen minutes searching web leads trying to track connections between Sinisay, Blaz, and the Qontaqian SG—Senden Geres, the military research facility that hunted powers—before Seiti held up an urgent hand. "Someone senses us." Her lids were half closed, as if she reached within.

"Hold that thought." Ilan brought up a map of her brain sensors and tapped keys. He examined grids closely.

The others brought their faces close to look with him.

"I don't think anyone identified us," Ilan said with relief.

"I agree," Gisli said. "No sign of reverse tracking."

"Let's find a different route."

They finally hit firewalls too robust for even Ilan or Gisli, not to mention Tlalit and Merne whose uncanny surveillance abilities Yanda had seen first-hand during their escape from Sheffed.

"I know of an old government IT room seldom used, on underground levels deep under Dondar," Gisli said. "I pulled codes from clerks' minds before I was discovered and became a fugitive with you all." He grinned. Beri laid a companionable hand on his shoulder.

"Let's try it when we go to the city tomorrow to buy Seiti her ENAC?" Ilan suggested. Seiti's eyes brightened. She lifted off the headset.

Ilan accepted it with a wink, his fondness obvious. "Let's start on Grethon from there. Unknown Space is harder to penetrate but also may give us an indirect conduit to the information we need about the rest."

Tenali strode down the long room, his usual rough renegade space-garb jingling and creaking. "I can help with that."

As always, Yanda's heart beat fast at the sight of him, sensing his mind, his heart, his essence.

"I'm curious if what Gisli and I have been exploring is close to what you have, Ten." When her partner's son drew near, Tlalit pulled him into a sideways hug.

He returned the embrace fondly, having known her most of his life.

She brought up a holographic screen and typed information.

Arsat and Bend arrived with Zami and he ran to Yanda, arms held up. She swept him into the air.

When Yanda, Ilan and the two children arrived back at the treehouse, Vatu was nowhere in sight. Yanda had looked forward to seeing her. She sent out a mind-search, calling to her.

Vatu answered from Vashal. "I've been working with the circle." She sounded excited. She'd expressed many times how she'd love to experience the great mind-meld with the elves in the pyramid above Shalt.

"I'm glad," Yanda said. "Are you tired yet? Did you eat?"

"They fed us, yes." Vatu seemed on a sort of high. "I think we will break for the night but not quite yet. Everything okay with you?"

"Yes. Lots to fill you in on." Yanda hugged herself, realizing how much she cherished sharing deep parts of her life and new revelations with Vatu. She hoped they always would.

Late that night, after a light supper that Ilan fetched from the elven kitchens, Seiti lay on Yanda's bed, drawing. "So we'll go to Sheffed tomorrow and get my ENAC?"

Yanda marked her place in an old-fashioned volume made of parchment-like *plaz* that she'd found in the elven library, a tree with platforms spiraling up numerous levels, a special shield around it to keep out dampness. The text was an ancient Earth novel called "Davinci Code" which intrigued Yanda no end.

"Yep. Sheffed and Dondar," Yanda responded.

Seiti's eyes shone with excitement for their planned journey to the city. Yanda wrapped an arm around her and gave her a hug, happy to be focusing on her daughter's needs and wants, happy to see her anticipating a shopping trip, able to be a child. She just hoped her having her own device didn't lead to worry and danger.

CHAPTER

13

At dawn, Yanda and the others stood in the field where the Sarsefi roosted, looming fifty feet in height, its long elegant lines, rounded, cobalt blue with pale insets along dividing panels, caught orange-gold morning light.

Decru strode from the cavern where he dwelt, sharing the underground labyrinth with the Great Stone, Shalt. The sky above him was still dark. Shouma was coming along as well. They wanted the strongest powers near Seiti when they left the protection of the elves' dome.

The elves had decided to take an old road, seldom used, that headed northwest out of Rotoul, briefly nearing the coast, then crossing desert plains to Sheffed. Yanda would be seeing a northeast part of the continent she'd never been to.

She held Zami's hand. He could barely contain himself as a grandiose land rover trundled toward them from a tunnel beneath the bunker, Tlalit in the driver seat.

Nine passengers climbed in and settled. Zami jumped up and down in his window seat, eager to see more of the planet. Seiti sat beside him, more sedate but eyes shimmering as she gazed out. The rover engaged its magnetic field, lifted off the ground and started on its way.

Little changed as, beyond the Sarsefi, they passed through the edge of the dome. Sparse foliage gave onto sea grasses as they approached the coastline. After glimpses of blue sea, they turned west and the terrain became bleak. Yanda saw low mountains in the distance, and farther off, the tops of the highest buildings in the city of Dondar. Sheffed must be hidden by hills.

"Are those mountains over the tunnels where we escaped from Dondar?" Yanda asked. "Well, they must be, unless there are further mountains."

"The tunnels go under there, yes," Merne answered. "Our continent is fairly narrow so there's just the one small mountain range that ends in Vashal."

Yanda had never wanted to return to Dondar after her long captivity there—kept from her daughter, raising her son in a single room of the Citadel his first year, unable to communicate with anyone from her past. But, at last she was ready. She even wanted to see the building in which they'd been held, now from a position of freedom, to show her children. Would they walk inside? Maybe she'd return with the rest of the fems. Of the ten fems held in that single long room, monitored day and night by spy mages, only she and Shouma were on this excursion.

Scattered buildings began to appear, mostly low rounded structures that could take the high winds of the desert. Soon slovenly hotels and bars signaled their approach to the rough fringe of Dondar known as Sheffed.

Buildings grew closer together and Yanda recognized the areas around Merne's apartment where they'd taken refuge in their escape. She saw the market street with vendor stalls.

"Look, Zami." She pointed. "We carried you in a pack, in that market place. When we first met Merne!"

His elven half-sister, a hundred years older than him, gave him a grin.

Zami stared down the street to the busy vendor stalls and turned his face up to Yanda. "You probably don't remember, Button. You were very little."

Seiti gazed as well. She slipped her hand into Yanda's next to her. "You haven't told me much about that. Being captured. Held," she whispered.

Yanda slipped her arm around her. "We will. We'll talk about it all. I promise." She had avoided the subject, mostly because it made her stomach hurt. That was when she deserted her daughter.

She wished Vatu were here. In fact, she wished Chin, the Jejods, all of the fems could be there to reminisce with her, painful as it was. They would have to come back. Vatu had stayed behind, to continue at Vashal, learning to hold the protective dome over Rotoul, and to draw energy from nature as well as give it back.

"I took you on a detour to walk memory lane," Tlalit remarked from the front. "Now we'll proceed to the big stores at the northernmost edge, supplied by the spaceport." She seemed to enjoy this duty as tour guide.

The impressive semi-military looking cross-country vehicle drew a lot of eyes along the shabby streets. Signs of wealth increased as they approached the boundary to the desert closest to the spaceport. Hotels grew, large restaurants sprang up, and multi-level shopping areas offered products of every kind on wall-signs that shifted, shimmering, building images from one side to the other. Zami and Seiti watched all this, as did Decru, seated at the front by the passenger window. It had been a while since he'd traveled into cities, he'd remarked as he took in the sights.

"Gisli?" Tlalit said.

In a middle section, Gisli had a miniature schematic of all the shopping areas and parking structures. Holographic screens stretched in front of him. "Forward to the next intersection, left then right," Gisli said. "Let's take the underground entrance. It'll say SP103. There's a garage and it also connects to an old military tunnel that will get us quite far into Dondar after."

"Perfect." Merne, sitting between Tlalit and Decru in the front seat, had small screens similar to Gisli's open all around her. I'm thinking we need to set a higher cloaking. I'm sensing an increase in surveillance this way."

Morning light shifted into the darkness of an underground garage as they descended a wide ramp. The gate lifted and they slid past a toll booth where the guard appeared to be asleep standing. The large vehicle looped down three levels. It pulled into a space far from other passenger *gallihoes, serstrops,* and *sedpods.* Nearby, a black square hinted at a tunnel. Yanda suspected not everyone could see it. They opened doors and piled out. Gisli, looking at a wrist hologram, led the way. "We want to get a lift over here."

Seven levels up, they followed a crowd along a carpeted hallway. Zami stared as wall plaz protruded with animal scenes and other eye-catching motifs. Some were ads, some purely art. She picked Zami up, wanting to help him contain some of his excitement, or to share it with him.

Decru drew close to a symbol that enlarged, shifted and closed in on itself to become a seashell and then an octopus. The old elf stared, seeming to derive special meaning from it, until they were almost out of sight of him. Then he was next to Yanda again.

Several buildings over, reached by connecting skyways, they came to the massive tech store Tlalit had in mind. Gisli's eyes brightened, lips parted in a small "o" as he took in the products constantly shifting in cascades throughout the seemingly unending interior. Lists on the walls told what could be obtained from storage. Screens high above showed the purposes of products from miniscule chips to towers of hardware, and clouds of amorphous capability. The compact Tellotian with his kind, deep plum-brown face, noticed Zami watching his reaction to the place and grinned. "Quite a lot to contemplate, isn't it, little man?"

Zami nodded. "I don't even know what most of it is."

"Oh, good things, my friend. Many I've never seen. They can do a lot."

Yanda watched one and then another, eyes grazing the enormous moving scene, having no idea where to begin searching for the ENAC her daughter wanted until she realized Seiti was not in the group. She moved down the aisle, Zami in her arms, mind sending out a call to her daughter. "Where are you?" She felt her and followed, rising to the floor above on an escalator, unaware the rest of the group straggled behind her.

At the far side of the expansive next level, she spotted Seiti, alone, gazing up at a screen. An ad for Tiklet shifted to scenes of marvels at the school, then showed the surrounding area.

Yanda whipped her head around, seeking Ilan. The rest of the group clustered close behind her. "Stop them. Stop her from getting any messages," she said into the others' minds. She knew between them they could break the spell Seiti seemed to be under.

Ilan pushed forward. "Let me read them first, see what might be coming through." He stepped in front of Seiti, blocking the screen from her view, and pressed his hands to her head. Yanda, in his mind, felt him take a snapshot of Seiti's recent thoughts. Then he gave a nod to Shouma and Decru.

Luckily, no one was around as the three moved to a couch. The elders searched for any thoughts that might have been inserted into her mind by what had been projected on the screen. Yanda would ask what they found later.

"How?" she whispered to Ilan. "How can they be advertising Tiklet? A secret school on Blaz that abducts children with powers? But it wasn't the Tiklet on Blaz. It was on Mir or somewhere with beautiful beaches."

Gisli moved close and subtly ran fingers along the inside of his hand. She was sure he checked the source of the ad; it had already changed.

"A decoy? I don't know. Definitely something sinister." Ilan concentrated.

"Are you storing the information from Seiti's mind?" she asked.

"I did. An imprint of what she took in and what she gave out."

"You mean she communicated with someone?" Yanda's blood froze.

"Let's don't jump to conclusions. I have to analyze it." He put an arm around her waist and they moved toward the others, Gisli coming with them, apparently having gotten all he could from the screen history.

Yanda was glad to see Seiti's face calm and conscious as she chatted with Shouma.

"Let's get that ENAC and then some lunch," Ilan suggested.

The ENACs were among the high-end, portable computing devices on the third floor of the store. Seiti's eyes lit up as she took in the varying colors, shapes, and sizes.

Gisli shyly took the girl's hand. "Can I show you one that's come out recently? I think it's suited to your skills, and it transforms. You can make it look like anything. A stuffed animal..." His eyes crinkled as he led the girl two rows over.

Ilan followed close behind, anxious to see them as well. Yanda and Zami tagged along.

Seiti caressed the surface of a small ENAC and colors shifted, leaving a path where her fingers touched. It was immediate love. "How do they keep people from shoplifting, if you can make it look like anything, a briefcase or a hat?" She giggled.

"I'm sure sensors read the codes at check-out," Gisli surmised.

A sales bot sidled up with a gliding step. For a while, bots had mimicked humanoids perfectly but that became a major issue. Now they were kept distinctly manufactured looking, with whimsical heads like gumdrops on the shoulders of practical *plaz* torsos replete with drawers for parts, dials, and meters. "Can I help you?" its pleasant monotone voice asked.

Gisli and Ilan peppered the droid with technical questions.

Seiti, with her hand to the ENAC's surface, named a string of facts with numbers about the elegant device in a worshipful tone.

Ilan and Gisli listened, spellbound by her eloquent fact-stream.

At the end, Seiti said, "This will suit me fine. Please obtain it for me," she requested of the bot. "The Mendon model with oceanic color scheme. I have chips." She held out her arm to show a patch for currency exchange.

As if on cue, Tlalit joined them. She pushed down Seiti's arm, saying mildly, "We have it covered. I'll meet you at the main checkout, base floor."

Minutes later, the group walked past purchase lines, Tlalit carrying the item in a plain plaz bag along with a few selections of her own. Out in the mall hallway, she pulled out the ENAC 420 and handed it to Seiti, who danced with it twirling, looking like any happy eight-year-old with a new toy.

In his quiet, unassuming way, Gisli said, "I saw they have a Tellotian café in the next building over. It's…people like the food of my planet. It has lots of tropical fruit and coconut. Some is spicy but it doesn't have to be."

"I'm for it," Beri said.

Everyone agreed they wanted to try the food of Gisli's native planet.

The décor in Café Tellot was prime colors with beach motifs. A mountain with a volcano spewing lava dominated the back wall. Tiki roofs lined the serving area, and tables had tropical animal shapes. Seiti chose a tall fuchsia drink.

Yanda suggested they try the tofu pocket bread packed with strips of mango and sauteed pepper. They sat at a long whale-shaped table and shared their tropical delights.

Yanda asked, "Are we all going under Dondar with Gisli?" sending the message into her companions' minds. She especially aimed the question at Tlalit and Merne. The two elves had spent a year gathering intel around Dondar while setting up the ten fems' escape. They knew nearly as much as Gisli about the workings of the city and its borough, Sheffed.

"I think that's not necessary," Gisli responded before taking an enormous bite of a Tellot burger, stacked high with roasted peppers and purple sauteed onions. Chewing, he sent the mind-message, "It'll be best to go at night with as few as possible."

Yanda looked around, about to ask what they'd do until then when she noticed Merne and Shouma appeared strained, eyes weary. Both were as good as Vatu and Ilan at holding disguises but this large a group over an extended period of time had to be taxing. "Should we pick out a hotel for the night?" she asked.

It was no surprise to any of them when Tlalit said, "That's done. I did a lot of research on Prok's underground to find the least monitored accommodations."

Beri said, "I'm not sure how unobtrusive if would be to arrive in the Beast, though." She quirked a half-grin.

"It's close. We can walk," Tlalit said.

Gisli said, "Let's move the jeep lower. We can find a place no one goes and shield it." He and Beri rose.

Tlalit got up as well and the three left the café, Tlalit sending the location into Merne's mind before she left.

Yanda ordered a couple of extra pocket breads to go,

along with sweet coconut chips and other snacks which she shoved into her shoulder pack. They would be set for the evening if they wanted to stay in.

CHAPTER

14

The group proceeded down alleys, avoiding larger streets, still disguised as ordinary Terlondians. Their biggest worry was anyone spotting Seiti. Without the protection of the elven dome, spies could be watching even from a satellite outside the planet's atmosphere.

Merne opted to lead the way; invisible and shielded to the hilt, she could scan ahead for hostile probes. Seiti tripped along behind her, seemingly without a care in the world, hugging her new ENAC which now looked like a stuffed sea horse. Shouma and Decru flanked her, riding in float-chairs. They could have been grandparents fondly surrounding the eight-year-old girl. Ilan, Yanda, and Zami played the parents and younger son, bringing up the rear.

Few denizens populated the alleys anyway, though supply carriers occasionally hummed through, forcing them to one side.

Their route ended up in front of a funky, art deco façade of Hotel Dorador. Yanda liked its lowkey atmosphere compared with lavish high rises closer to the great mall. Shrubberies bordered walkways on either side.

Tlalit arrived at the same time they did, Beri and Gisli behind her. Looking like a tall school teacher in glasses, a cloud of hair hiding her ears, her unusual peach skin tone glamoured to a beige tan, she ran up the front steps. The others moved along a path to the side to wait.

Soon they had passkeys to a side entrance and four rooms toward the back of the hotel. In no time, most were climbing stairs. Decru chose the lift and Shouma joined him, pulling Zami onto her lap on her float-chair.

The rooms were in a row on the eighth floor. Yanda and Seiti met Zami at the elevator. Lifting her tired son, she carried him to their room down the hall. Inside, she flipped on a light. Evening sent glowering orange-red through the single window.

Zami struggled to get down and the kids ran to the two beds and flopped onto fanciful bedspreads of unknown germs.

Yanda called to them, "Wait, come, let me disinfect." She thought, *if I can change cells, surely I can cleanse this room.*

Since her recent time underwater with Decru, she'd sensed new powers lurking.

She'd mentioned it and Decru had responded, "It's most likely your Xentu blood coming into maturity."

Now she closed her eyes and tapped into that new part of her. Starting at the door, she sent a wave slowly around the hotel room, into every crevice and under each surface. It took surprisingly little energy. She crossed the beds area and soon reached full circle. She opened her eyes.

Seiti and Zami watched her carefully. They had entered her mind as if to detect her method and be able to emulate it. Yes, it was a lesson. She could teach her children. Her heart raced as she bent and hugged them to her.

"That should do it. Feel free to jump on." She grinned, taking in the admiration in their eyes. She was so often awed their abilities, it was only fair to be reciprocated. And she needed so much to know they were learning to keep themselves safe. Every day taught her that.

Seiti crawled onto a bed, settled pillows behind her and opened her ENAC 420. A button on the side raised a cushion under it that molded to her lap. Lights stirred within it and holographic screens popped up.

Ilan spoke into Yanda's mind. "I'm next door to you. If it's okay, I'll monitor what Seiti does on her device." He seemed to know the instant she woke the ENAC.

"That's best," Yanda answered, "for now."

"Of course. Only until danger is gone," he assured her with an extra press of the words into her mind.

Zami quietly watched his sister, hugging Yanda's leg.

"What's up, Button?" Yanda asked stroking his hair, then sitting at the end of the other bed and pulling him to her.

"When do I get one?" he asked in almost a whisper.

Of course, he wanted one. "You didn't say a word when we were in the store." She pulled his small device from her backpack and handed it to him.

He accepted it with a grin. "Maybe I learn more and then you could get me one."

What did I do to deserve such a reasonable son, she asked herself as she pulled him onto the bed next to her. A tap came on the door.

Yanda got up to answer, seeing Merne through the plaz of the carved door, made to imitate old Earth wood.

Trees were rarely used for furniture or paper, only for nature appreciation and sequestering carbons.

Merne stepped in. "I thought Zami might like to have this guy for a while." She took her little monkey friend, Tuk-tuk, from his tiny pack. Inside the pouch where she kept him hidden was a miniature Sultan's chair.

He bounded across the room to Zami.

"Let's give him something to climb on, shall we?" Merne concentrated on one side of the room and a structure manifested from floor to ceiling. Lines resembling plunka sticks formed intricate crisscrossing runways.

Zami sent a ball of light through, giggling as Tuk-tuk chased it with gleeful chittering.

Seiti watched, then turned her eyes back to her screens.

"Thank you" Yanda said to Merne. "Great idea."

"You're most welcome, Tuk-tuk needs it as well. I'm beat. I'll sleep soon."

Yanda touched the elven woman's arm. "I'm not surprised. That was tiring, I'm sure."

"A larger group than I'm used to disguising, especially over a prolonged period. But not all that..." Merne's eyes drifted around the room. She sniffed the air. "Did you cleanse this room?"

"I did. You can tell?" Yanda's eyes brightened with fascination.

"I can indeed." Merne pressed fingers to Yanda's temple and Yanda went directly to that new place in her.

"Do a little now, would you?" Merne asked, hand resting on Yanda's head.

Yanda dropped back into the state from which she changed their room, eliminating toxicity from cleaners, bacteria, even bad vibes.

Merne's mouth opened forming an O. She sighed. "That's fabulous. Conversion or removal?" She seemed to ponder. "You're replacing, drawing from elsewhere. That's why it smells sweeter in here."

"Like Bonden's apparatus to help Vatu breathe," Yanda said, pondering her own accomplishment. "I think I also dismantled a listening device. There could have been more. It kind of did itself, this cleansing. I just set it in motion."

"Was it tiring? Do you think you could do our rooms? I don't sense I have this ability…" Merne grinned… "yet."

Yanda called to Ilan by thought. "Can you come in with the kids for a little while?"

"You going to transform my room, too?" he asked and she felt the smile in his mind.

"Of course."

Yanda and Merne first cleansed Ilan's room which he shared with Decru.

Decru said, "I should have thought of that. Marvelous." And helped.

Then they cleansed Beri and Gisli's.

"Decru's staying with Ilan?" Beri asked, eyes too eager.

Yanda scowled. "You'd better leave him alone."

He gave her a half-contrite, half-stubborn expression.

"Beri." Her tone held warning.

"Alright. Alright."

Last they started in on the room Merne, Tlalit, and Shouma shared. As Yanda performed her magic, the other three followed, trying to sense her technique.

Shouma beamed at her with approval. "I like it. You'll show me." It was not a question.

When Yanda returned to her room, Ilan asked, "How many tracking devices?"

Yanda shrugged. "I'm not sure."

"I wish you'd saved some."

She slapped his shoulder. "Ingrate."

He half-smiled. "But you did a great thing destroying them. Thank you."

"I see you added features to the structure," she said, noticing windows of light appearing and disappearing.

"Oh, we've had a great time. Can I stay?" Ilan gave her a hang-dog beg.

"A little while," she said, settling against pillows with a small satellite version of her ENAC.

Late that night, Yanda lay in a bed she shared with Zami, letting Seiti have her own.

This trip had not gone as smoothly as Yanda had imagined. She'd wanted the shopping excursion to bring delight to her daughter. But then that screen drew Seiti with its ad for Tiklet which Yanda couldn't get out of her mind, suspecting screens everywhere might talk to Seiti without her knowing.

It was not long before Ilan tapped on her mind, clearly attuned to her spiraling worries. "I've examined all that Seiti saw and thought during her time in front of the screen. She's clear. No subliminal messages. No communication from her."

"But what drew her to it?" she thought back to him, head on her pillow.

"Maybe she heard the name Tiklet from it."

"So the school gave her acute hearing? Some implant?"

"Or it's a Xentu skill," Ilan suggested.

Of course, Yanda thought. Everyone but she always thought of that.

"We have to see what Gisli found when he gets back," Ilan said.

"They've left? Who all went?" Why hadn't she sensed them leaving?

"Just a few. Merne, Tlalit, Gisli, and Beri."

"The old folks are worn out," Yanda said, smiling with fond thoughts of Decru and Shouma in their float chairs on the way to the hotel.

"We'd better sleep," Ilan said, though Yanda suspected he'd be right back on his device.

Later, as she was finally drifting off to sleep, she felt Zami shake her.

"Seiti's on the roof," he said.

Yanda sat up, staring at him. "Can you bring us there?" She was already out of bed, pulling on a jacket and pocketed canvas pants over her nightgown. She dressed Zami quickly and he took her hand. Instantly they were surrounded by roof garden, looking out over low walls at city lights. Yanda spotted her daughter gazing at the cityscape from a central bench.

After a brief hesitation, Yanda sat close to her daughter, facing out, breathing in the night air. "Whatcha doing up here, sweetie?" She took Seiti's small hand in hers.

"I was curious what it might be like. A sign said 'roof garden'," Seiti answered. She didn't seem resentful of the intrusion. "And I wanted to think."

Zami made a circuit around the garden paths of the roof, then came to settle on Yanda's other side.

"Did you climb the stairs, or pop yourself up here?"

"I popped," Seiti said, grinning briefly. Her smiles never seemed to last long.

"I didn't know you could do that," Yanda said.

"When Merne transported me—when I was conscious—I was in her mind and studied how she did it. A couple of times I did it with Zami, too." Seiti pulled back her hand and folded it with the other in her lap.

"It's beautiful from up here," Yanda commented.

"Lights always are. You don't know what's under or behind them," Seiti said, serious, then barked a small laugh, more like a cough. "Kind of a dark thought."

Yanda smiled. "It's so true, though." Then she asked, "Did that screen in the tech store call to you?"

Seiti gazed out without answering, eyes unfocused.

Yanda feared she shouldn't have brought it up.

Finally, Seiti shrugged, ever so lightly. "I don't know."

Taking another slow breath, Yanda plunged in further. "We've never talked about this but I was told you were being prepared. That kids at Tiklet were being made into…"

Seiti's eyes were on her mother. "Into what?"

Another breath. "Um…weapons." Yanda studied Seiti's face as her daughter took a long time to respond. When she didn't, Yanda asked, "Were you ever told anything like that?"

Seiti brought her knees up and rested her chin on a palm. "I guess you could say there were signs. We were sometimes pitted against each other."

"What kind of pitted?" Yanda asked, imagining anything from hand-to-hand combat to video games.

"We had to spy and find out things about other students. I didn't like that. They seemed to make us do that against someone they thought we liked."

Yanda put her arm around Seiti, pulling her close. The night had grown chilly, with winds crossing the hotel roof. Zami put a heat bubble around them.

"Thanks, brother. Good job," Seiti reached across Yanda and patted the little boy. She went on, "Later they had me try to find out things about people far away. About you especially. They wanted to know everything about you. At first it was hard to find out anything since you weren't on Alland anymore. I never knew where you went." Her lower lip trembled, caught in the floodlights that shone on vines crawling the walls. "When I couldn't find anything, they started telling me things I know now aren't true. There was a guy who would come on the screen. They'd let him talk to me. He..." Seiti's voice trailed off, features bunched in an effort not to cry.

Yanda hugged her harder. "Was it Krid? Kridenit?"

"The guy who kidnapped you? Show me what he looks like."

With a sour belly, Yanda brought up a memory of his face, in his office on Farn, and his lavish rooms at the Citadel: thin face, sharp handsome features, dark close clipped beard. His flinty eyes curdled her insides. Reluctantly she gave the image into her daughter's mind. The man who thought he was Zami's father. Zami reached and took his mother's hand. She kissed his head.

"That's him," Seiti said.

Yanda made a growling sound in her throat as she gazed at the stars, trying to sense if she and Zami could protect Seiti up there from incoming messages or signals Seiti herself might send out, inadvertently. She assumed inadvertently. It was hard to know if her daughter might act as an enemy. She could have had her mind turned against them and be acting. Yanda shook that thought away. "What did he say to you? If you want to tell." She braced herself.

"I think he was grooming me. He'd be coming to visit, he said, and would bring me gifts."

Yanda ached to think her daughter even knew of abusers grooming victims.

"It's okay. It's okay," Yanda whispered. "I'm here." She pushed a strand of Seiti's hair out of her eyes. "We're so much smarter now. No one can do this to us again. Pull us apart. Hold us captive."

"Are you sure?" Seiti asked, voice hoarse.

Zami, who'd been sitting at Yanda's side, crawled onto her lap and snuggled closer to Seiti. He had uncanny sensors for distress.

Seiti surprised her by saying, "I think they had us spy on each other because they wanted us to be good spies. Maybe they would have had me spy on Krid, if he took me away. But also…"

Zami snuggled in her lap, head against her chest, eyes on his half-sister, Yanda waited for more.

Seiti didn't go on right away. Finally, she said, "Also to make us feel alone."

Yanda shivered, holding onto both her kids.

"At night, I felt my thoughts close in, missing you. I cried too much and they gave me sleep drugs. They said I was losing weight. 'Not achieving optimal weight' was the way they put it, the school doctors. We had to see them every week. Them and the psychologists."

Yanda rubbed Seiti's thin sleeve, squeezing Zami with her other arm. She wanted to take her daughter's memories somewhere pleasant. "You stayed in a very nice house though?"

Seiti turned wide eyes to her, a crease in her brow. "Nice. Yes. Rich. Comfortable. I tried to make my room personal, but had no pictures. Of you. Or anything from home. They controlled what I could look up. I made drawings. Not very good ones."

Yanda said, "I had no photos of you either. That was torture. They took my devices away and wouldn't let me get onto anything electronic."

"Did they take your chip?" Seiti asked, touching her temple.

"Oh yes. Right from the start, Krid had that out."

"They took mine, too, at the school. I'm sure they grubbed through it." Then Seiti asked, "Does Zami have a knowledge chip?"

"No. Zamani won't hear of it." Yanda smiled down at her. "I understand. But you know, when I lived with the Neyla, Mnenu taught me to store images. Vatu can do it too and showed me more. You can then put them into AI when you have a chance and make them…digital. Physical."

"Now that's *ziprit*," Seiti said, enjoying a shared moment with Yanda over the outback word that had gotten popular on Alland when they both still lived there.

"I'll teach you," Yanda said.

"You have to," Seiti said. "You know, for all their tech, there's so much mind stuff they don't know, so much so that they couldn't even detect it."

"That's why they want people like us. The Blaz, the Sinisay, some Qontaqis."

"You're shielding, right?" Ilan asked from his room three floors below. "I'm not hearing you but I caught words in AI."

"Darn. I thought I was," she answered him. Then to

Seiti and Zami she said, "When we get back to Rotoul, we need to test our shielding. I think we can all learn to do more. Let's get back to bed. I think it's starting to mist up here."

Light rain began to fall as they ran for shelter, then transported instantly to their room, laughing.

CHAPTER

15

The next morning's light seemed to arrive way too quickly. Yanda's eyes felt scratchy as Zami wiggled and then sat up. She put an arm around him and lay thinking. What had the four found out on their trip to the bowels of Dondar?

A knock came at the door and she wished it was Vatu. She missed her.

"We're going for breakfast," Ilan said into her mind. She looked through the walls to see his tall, sturdy form already dressed and ready.

The ten trooped to a nearby café. On the walk, Yanda asked into Tlalit and Merne's minds, "Did you find anything out?"

"Let's wait 'til the drive home. The Beast is the most secure," Tlalit responded.

In Sheffed, one was much more likely to find an unusual variety of diners than in Dondar, so they disguised themselves lightly, less worried about drawing attention.

Surveillance was far lower in the borough than in the mall. All types left the spaceport to come into the rough and un-refined ghetto that bordered the north end of Dondar. Some ended up staying. Others just passed through.

Such variety was the case at the Blue Mirrdoo, a sham-bling single-story café that occupied the better part of a city block, next to a liquor store and repair shops. The group decided on a back corner in a rear room. Yanda glanced around. Appearance wasn't the only notable diversity. Voices ranged from high fluting to low rumbling tones.

Once they were seated around three tables shoved to-gether, Zami watched one particular small man until the wide-faced fellow with pointed ears winked at him. Not elf, Yanda thought, but some mix. She thought of Tenali, rugged space pilot. He hadn't come along on this excur-sion. He seemed to be keeping distance from her. Or was it the other way around?

"I think we should go by the Citadel," Shouma said out of nowhere as they studied menus on holographic screens that popped up before each of them.

Yanda had wondered why Shouma seemed so bent on returning to where they'd long been held captive. She'd mentioned it in the Balyou underground as well. Yanda had resisted the idea vehemently. Now, she realized she was ready to tackle it, to reduce the Citadel's power to haunt her. It might help Seiti to know where her mother had been kept, where Zami was born.

"Let's go by the shop where I was apprenticed, too," Beri requested.

"And your quarters, Gisli. Do you mind if we see that area?" Yanda asked.

Gisli shrugged, his smile a mere press of the lips.

He doesn't want to go, she thought.

"Let's do a full tour," Tlalit said.

They ordered all sorts of *zad*-flour pancakes—a rare treat limited to Fallan enclaves that cropped up in cities around the universe. They scooped fillings, fruity and savory, out of dishes passed around.

Halfway through the meal, and on their second round of *kaffe*, Decru surprised them by getting up and walking over to the small pointy-eared man who had so interested Zami. Decru pulled out a chair and sat by him and they spoke for some time.

Yanda shared a raised eyebrow with Ilan and others.

Beri could not stop fidgeting, clearly too curious to contain himself.

When they'd enjoyed enough *kaffe* and breakfast, Tlalit did her usual subtle coverage of the bill with a sweep of credits onto the same screen that had offered the menu. She then left with Gisli to fetch the Beast. Since they'd traveled lightly, their small bags were tucked under seats or hanging from chairs.

Yanda peered through the tinted vehicle windows as they left the scarred urban edifices of Sheffed and entered the main, and only city of Terlond. Dondar was not a remarkable metropolis, in terms of the universe, but everyone in this group had an intense history with it. Common shops lined the streets. Dondarians, a rather conservative lot, peopled the sidewalks and busied the noonday streets with various transports. First, they came to the northern garret where Gisli had been housed with the other military, and Beri's rooming house for apprentices. It was a dreary few blocks, gray and uninspiring.

"Nice digs," Ilan said, jabbing Gisli in the ribs. The two

had grown close over the technologies they both lived and breathed.

"Don't you know it." Gisli returned the elbow-dig.

"Oh, I do. I've lived in very similar on Qontaq," Ilan responded.

"I saw them," Yanda said. "Everywhere they seem to come up with the same uninspired institutional look." Her mind was dragged unwilling to those horrific moments when she and Ilan had searched for Bonden, and found her.

"Do you want to get out and see anything?" Tlalit asked. "Maybe go to the café where you two met?"

"I think not," Beri said. He turned to Gisli. "You?"

"Nah. It's all here." He tapped his head.

They crossed into the center of the small city. Merne pointed out parks added since the concentrated effort to clean away the toxic air, helped behind the scenes by the elves who never wanted to draw attention to themselves but desired to return the planet to health.

"Now we're approaching Beri's former work," Tlalit said as she navigated through noonday traffic. "I came to see you here, you know." She glanced in the mirror at Beri in the seat behind her.

"You did?" Beri asked, surprised.

"Oh yeah. I looked different, of course, but I watched over you."

"Huh." Beri appeared to sink within himself.

Yanda peered in the shop to see if she'd catch a glimpse of the fat pompous man who'd lorded over Beri those many months. Glare on the window allowed no penetration for the others but Yanda could easily see through to the belts and wallets, and the red-faced gob-shite who shouted at a new apprentice.

"Yuck," she said into Beri's mind and she gave him a picture of what she was seeing.

"Yuck is right," he responded. "Poor sucker."

Tlalit turned down an avenue lined with mansions. "And now we approach the Citadel."

As the Grecian arches of the Citadel grounds came into view, Yanda braced herself. They drew close to the front where Yanda read a sign under the arched entrance. "Garden School."

What a laugh, she thought, but then she heard children laughing, and saw them playing in the expansive yard. She realized the prison towers had been removed from the corners of the block. Could this be a happy place now?

"It's been turned into a school?" she asked.

"Yep, I was saving that as a surprise," Merne said.

"You sure did," Yanda answered. She felt resentful that she hadn't known as soon as Merne knew. She also felt suspicious. She ducked her head to peer up at the three-story inner sanctum that now must house school administration. Her heart was hammering. She asked Ilan, "Can you tell anything about it?" She imagined Krid back there, turning the Citadel into a school like Tiklet. It would be just his style.

"I know what you're thinking," Tlalit said. "Krid is not here. It is not…that kind of school. And we are monitoring him."

"Then why can he visit Seiti at Tiklet?" she thought.

A stunned silence ran through the vehicle.

Then Tlalit said, "This vehicle is well shielded, but let's resume this, have a full meeting when we're out of this city."

Seiti turned to her mom, catching her thought. She reached over Zami and touched Yanda's shoulder, a hint of a smile on her lips.

Yanda nodded. She'd shown Seiti her memories of the place.

"I remember about the mage spies," Seiti said into Yanda's mind. "I know you couldn't come to me."

Yanda realized she had held that guilt tightly, asking herself relentlessly, "Could I have done more? Got away sooner? Communicated somehow?"

Zami wiggled closer to her and Yanda was glad to touch both her children, sense their presence. She had to do anything she could to keep them close to her and safe. She must get stronger, learn more skills, be cleverer, she told herself, hammering the thought into the knots in her gut.

Tlalit called out, "Are we ready to go home?"

Yanda asked, "Can we see where the tunnels go under? There were skylights over that golden city."

"Sure." Tlalit turned to head east. "It's on our way. It's always been a park outside the city."

"Can we go into the tunnels some day?" Seiti asked.

"On another trip? Sure," Merne said. "We could take it backward from the edge of Rotoul."

Yanda pictured starting out from Rotoul and making their way back through the tunnels. "I think I'd like that. We should bring Zamani."

Why did she say that? Well, it was strange to think he hadn't been with them on that first journey. He'd been waiting in his elven forest to welcome them, to keep them safe. What would it be like to retrace the steps of their escape with him? Not all of them, of course. They would not have to rise through thirty feet of concrete to the Citadel, now a school. Would she want to see the hall she'd shared with nine fems, sometimes excruciatingly claustrophovi, where she'd given birth to Zami? Now full of children's laughter? "Is it a day school or residential?" she asked, looking directly at Merne, who seemed to have already known about it. "Are the kids from Dondar, or other places?"

Merne turned to look at her. "Day school. Poor kids from Sheffed. Part of city improvement."

Yanda looked back. She could still see the high luxurious center of what had been the Citadel, where Krid kept his lavish rooms, with their plush carpets, polished wood desks, and velvet curtains, where she'd climbed the curved stairs carrying Zami to present to "his father". So Krid thought. She'd been terrified that he'd take him. But she'd gotten him away.

Zami, perched on a bumper seat, watched for the park.

"You were a baby. You probably don't remember the journey under the city," Yanda said to him. "We took turns carrying you in my pack."

"I remember Tik and Jat flying up to the top of the gold building," he said. "unless I caught it in your memories. It seems real."

"I'm sure it is, little man." Yanda kissed his cheek.

"Here's the park," Tlalit announced, pulling to the side of an expanse of hilly land with Dondarians walking pets, jogging, or flying kites. In the distance, the forest of Rotoul and the mountains of Vashal should have been visible but the elves had kept up the protective dome, keeping the illusion of only marshlands in the distance. When would they feel safe enough to reveal their existence?

Tlalit parked at the curb and everyone poured out of the truck. Cut lawns gave way to higher grasses as they approached the center of the park, following Merne and Tlalit. Yanda saw through to tunnels several levels under the earth. Then she spotted the opening, like a city square, with the golden shiny buildings, catching half-light from the partially obscured sky-lights, thick plaz surrounded by small trees and foliage. Yanda remembered, during their escape through the tunnels, looking up and seeing tree branches waving. She remembered longing for the wind on her face after years in a single room in the Citadel.

The only others in this group who'd been on that trek were Beri, Gisli, Zami and Merne. Beri and Gisli were satisfied with a picture from her mind regarding how the strange and mysterious golden city looked from above. Merne already knew quite well what it looked like. But Zami and Seiti pushed through the scrub and knelt. Zami rubbed dirt away and pressed his face to the thick plaz.

Yanda followed her children, standing close.

Zami turned to her. "That's our city."

Something stirred in Yanda's insides, something electric as profound truth came to rest in her psyche, not yet clear but accepted.

"Let's don't draw too much attention, eh?" Merne said into their minds. She and Tlalit held back, asking the others to do the same.

Yanda knelt. "Right, Button. I get you." She held out her arms for him to come to her. "I think we'll know lots more about this soon." She felt the weight of impending conversations with her parents, with that moon being, Grethon, and with the Xentu. Were there any other Xentu? Or were her parents the only ones left.

Decru hovered close by under a willow, watching. When she caught his gaze, he nodded. Some confirmation came from him, nothing clear. That she would have answers soon, she thought he conveyed.

They tromped back across high grasses, then manicured ones, to the large jeep and piled back in for the drive out of the city.

CHAPTER

16

O kay, so you're going to share what you discovered last night?" Yanda asked, keenly aware that the subject had not been broached at any point that morning.

"Yeah, we can talk about it," Tlalit said as she drove them through the last of Sheffed's poorer outskirts. "The Beast has a unique system embedded to obscure the conversation, even thoughts and identities of those within."

"Though anyone can see us before we get in the vehicle," Beri pointed out. Aside to Shouma, he said, "Unless you were making us invisible in Dondar."

"When necessary," the elder Sonda responded.

"Seiti has not been visible to those outside our group since we left Rotoul," Merne added. "She was disguised in Tech Heaven and the cafés, of course."

"Is this really the time to talk about last night, though?" Tlalit asked, glancing in her rearview mirror at the two children who gazed out the window. "Or can it wait for the bunker where we have all our tech at hand, to answer questions and research further."

"It seems to me the children are very much a part of all this," Yanda said.

Decru and others nodded in agreement.

"Fine. Where do we start?" Tlalit shot looks at Merne, Gisli, and Beri who'd made the midnight foray with her into Dondar's underground networks.

Seiti glanced at her mom, then away. She wished she could be elsewhere, because she knew things she shouldn't know. And she knew how to hide that knowledge. She wished she hadn't discovered ways to obscure her mind quite so well, even from her mother and the others. Any thought she wanted them to find, she had to deliberately leave open, like bread crumbs, she was so used to keeping a steel door shut on her mind.

She was also far too good at finding out what she wanted to know. She had to hide that from Tlalit, and Ilan, who had tried very hard to scan all her skills, all the information that resided in her. She most regretted hiding the truth from Gisli. He was sincere and kind. Not that the others weren't. But they were less naive. He seemed like he would never think anything bad about anyone.

A discussion began about the discoveries of the night. Yanda listened for grand revelations about Melcraf, the strange smoke being, and her parents, connections to Blaz, and so on. But the palaver ended up to be disappointing, all network names and "we'll have to follow this code, that lead". It sounded like they'd laid some important groundwork but had found no true answers she could discern.

Yanda could not miss the tremor of unease that suddenly ran through Decru's mind at the front of the vehicle, where he sat between Merne and Tlalit. "You must bring Seiti to Shalt as soon as we arrive," he communicated urgently only to her.

His tone chilled her. "You've found out something?"

"I have, and it can't wait," he responded.

"Why are you keeping it secret?"

"Only I heard it," he said, and he was morose.

They said no more though Yanda held a sense of foreboding deep in her gut. Conversation dwindled as all watched desert, then coast flora, passing by until they reentered Rotoul through the dome's invisible barrier. They cruised past the towering Sarsefi. Tlalit brought the jeep to a stop in the turn-around near the small hill at the back of the bunker. Passengers debarked at the tunnel opening and Tlalit drove into the bowels of the elves' multi-level subterranean refuge.

"Come," Decru said quietly to Yanda.

"Can it wait—?" she started to say as Zami took her hand. She'd been picturing a nice family time in the treehouse upon their return.

"It can't," he mumbled and walked toward the caves.

Yanda rested her arm on Seiti's shoulder. To Ilan she said, "Could you keep Zami with you for a bit?"

Zami's eyes were big on her. She stroked his cheek.

Beri watched Decru's retreating back and glared at Yanda. "Aren't we going to meet?"

The journalist wants to get to Decru, she thought, and ignored him. Much more was afoot.

"Of course," Ilan said. "What do you think, little guy. Swim? Or…?"

"I'd like to swim," Seiti said, something testy in her voice.

"Decru has invited us…" Yanda didn't finish the sentence. She didn't know what to say that would seem natural.

"I don't want—" Seiti was cut off mid-sentence as she and Yanda were brought instantly to Decru in the cavernous caves. Shalt sent up an ice-blue glow at the center, shining from the fifty-foot maw.

The three stood together in blackness. Only a narrow shaft of light penetrated above them at the cave entrance.

"No!" Seiti struggled away from Yanda and ran toward the steep access road.

Decru was instantly in front of her. "Come, child," he said, putting light but firm hands on her arms.

"You heard my thoughts, didn't you?" Seiti hissed, squirming to get away. "You got something from that little man in the café, and you listened."

Yanda had never heard her daughter's voice hold such venom, had never seen hatred in her eyes like they held now as she twisted, trying to free herself from the elf elder.

Yanda's hand covered her mouth as she hurried toward them, giving Decru a troubled look.

"Shalt wants to heal her," Decru conveyed in mindspeak.

"I won't go!" Seiti screamed.

Yanda saw actual terror in her daughter's eyes, cast toward Shalt's glow.

"Why would she be afraid of Shalt?" Yanda asked Decru. "Unless…" She pictured Krid's encounter with the Great Stone that had overpowered him, the stone that had been his obsession since boyhood when his father had tried to dominate the stone, had blasted pieces from Shalt that wounded all elf civilization. Their attacks had left nuclear fallout contaminating Dondar and surrounding areas for generations. Was Krid lurking in her daughter's mind? Could he have been present, spying on them all this time since they brought Seiti back from Blaz? But how did everyone miss that? Unless Seiti's powers of obscuring were beyond all their talents.

"I think you may have hit the answer," Decru said ominously.

Shouma and Merne appeared next to them. Merne reached out and touched Seiti's shoulder, rendering her unconscious. She caught her inert body, gently bringing her to the ground as she knelt cradling her.

"She was right, though," Decru said. "I did obtain something from Bleens. The person I met at the Blue Mirrdoo. I don't think I would have penetrated her thoughts without it." He pulled back a sleeve to reveal a band snaking around his wrist. Light pulsed in it as if it were alive.

"How—?" A dozen questions circled in Yanda's mind. How did this Bleens tie in to her daughter? What was he?

"It wasn't easy for me to admit that I was out of my depth," Decru said, kneeling by Merne and Seiti. "I called him before we left yesterday. He traveled all night to be at the café in Sheffed in the morning."

Traveled all night? From somewhere on Terlond? Or off planet? Did it matter?

"Zami seemed quite drawn to him," Yanda said. "Is Krid inside Seiti's mind?"

She glanced at Merne who'd promised they were monitoring the monster.

"This is a discussion for more than us. But I don't think it's Krid," Merne said.

"Let's get onto Shalt's surface," Decru insisted.

As if to punctuate the suggestion, the stone rumbled, vibrating under their feet.

"Seiti said Krid came to her on monitors at Tiklet." Yanda's insides roiled as she struggled to make sense of what was happening with her daughter, her heart ready to break, anger boiling.

Shouma rested warm hands on her shoulders.

Yanda turned her head up to her abruptly, wanting to find comfort but unable. "You checked her. Ilan did, Decru did. Everyone examined her. Soni cleansed her. What is going on?" A sob hitched in her throat. "I thought you were all-powerful. So powerful." Her voice dwindled as anger gave in to bitter disappointment.

Shouma put her arms around her apprentice, resting her cheek to the top of Yanda's head. "*Cale bri tenna gee awsh mey annnnn,*" she whispered, holding the last sound as though in prayer.

Yanda let tears fall. "There's no hope. They really are stronger than any of us," she mumbled, turning her face into Shouma's richly embroidered kaftan.

"Nay. Nay," Shouma crooned.

Decru herded them across the cave's floor toward the Great Stone's gaping hole.

Merne easily carried the light eight-year-old girl in her arms.

Seiti had been terrified to approach Shalt, yet there they were, bringing her, unconscious, in its direction.

"What did you hear in Seiti's mind?" Yanda asked Decru as they stood looking down at the vast blue surface of the moon that never floated in the skies, caught inside a developing planet.

After a brief heartbeat, Decru answered, "I heard Seiti's thought, 'I wish I couldn't keep everyone out so thoroughly.' It worried me. Something in her tone. I believe your daughter is carrying a very big, very dark secret."

The idea unnerved Yanda but instead of prodding deeper into it, she asked, "What type of healing does Shalt have in mind? Do you know?"

"I surmise the kind that will allow her to share." Decru took Yanda's hand. "She has answers we need. Now."

His skin felt leathery, papery but warm. Leaving her hand in his, Yanda turned toward the elf woman. "Merne, you said it's not Krid in her. So...what? who?"

Merne did not answer.

Instead, Decru asked, "Are you ready to have things laid open?"

As their feet lifted off the ground, Yanda murmured, "I don't think my answer would make much difference."

They floated out over Shalt and downward.

It struck Yanda that, in the past, Zamani had been part of large moments with Shalt. But Seiti was not his kin, his blood. Was that the reason he was not there? She had no more time to ruminate. They were approaching Shalt's surface.

They lay, as before, pressed to Shalt's top side, barely curving, cold to the touch at first, heating wherever they touched. Yanda became instantly naked, as though the stone would tolerate no fabric separating them. She did not notice if others were bare as they fanned out from a central point where their heads nearly touched. Lying on her back, the Stone's energy filled her mind. She sensed Ash-don as well, and the elven circles. She was relieved to have their powerful force involved as she let the mind-meld shiver through her and settle.

"Here we are again," Shalt intoned. "We have been here before. Will it be different? Will we find the answers we need?"

They waited, sensing the Great Stone had more to say.

"Wake, little indomitable spirit," Shalt said, meaning her daughter.

Seiti's eyes opened. Yanda slid her fingers over Seiti's hand. The terror had gone from Seiti's eyes and she gazed calmly back.

Yanda wished Vatu were there. She always brought healing where needed. She detected Vatu's mind in the meld, sitting in the ring of stone seats high above them in the crystal pyramid.

"I'm here," Vatu said, sensing Yanda reaching for her.

"I love you," Yanda said to her. "I missed you."

"I love you, sister, and always miss you," Vatu assured her without hesitation.

"Seiti has been keeping part of her mind closed off. I wish you were here to—"

Suddenly the place where Yanda and Seiti had lain was empty. Decru sat up, looking around. Merne and Shouma crawled around. Yanda and her daughter were gone.

CHAPTER

17

Yanda tried to see through dense smoke. Panic rose as she sought breath. She forced herself to slow all her body processes. As she'd learned in the Jejod's cloud world, she adjusted her sight to penetrate the atmosphere. Her lungs strained for oxygen. As if she swam in *lanten* state, her lungs changed. She felt a prickling as she drew in the black smoke, light-headed at first but then adjusting. How was this possible? There was no oxygen in Unknown Space. For she knew somehow that she'd been drawn to Melcraf.

She took in the large room, like a theater. Features incrementally took form. She spotted Seiti sitting, untroubled, between her grandparents, Dal'an and Ebri. She struggled up from the cold shiny floor and stumbled to the closest seat a curved chair of black shiny material. No one came to help her, to welcome or comfort her.

There were others in the room. Were they really there, or an illusion? It seemed like nearly a hundred, dressed like her parents, dark austere clothing with high collars, narrow faces coldly elegant.

Voices bounced around the cavernous walls of the chamber.

Her parents and Seiti were some distance away. She wanted to run to her daughter but as yet felt unable, her legs shaking, stomach quaking.

She searched for Vatu and the rest, but could not find any of the mind-meld. "How were you able to pull us away?" she asked. "We were..." She stopped before telling who she'd been with, assuming they knew.

"Mama," Seiti said into her mind. "I was not able to tell you. They wouldn't let me."

"I understand, sweetie," she said, though she didn't.

"Do you want one of your friends here?" Dal'an asked, not entirely unkindly. "The Mingal, perhaps? I like her."

"Not if you're going to play games with her." Yanda was surprised to hear how stony her voice sounded. *Don't let me turn into my mother*, she thought.

"I've been here before, Mama." Seiti fidgeted with her fingers, eyes wide with contrition, seeming to beg that Yanda still love her.

"You really were dancing on the surface here, when my spirit came to you? How? I think I can breathe here due to *lanten* but how are you surviving?"

"She's all Xentu," Ebri broke in, rudely listening to what had, Yanda thought, been a private conversation between her and her daughter.

All Xentu. Yanda had always dodged questions of Seiti's conception, believing it was a careless night of partying, one where memories were lost after. She really had never known. Xentu? How could she have randomly, unknowingly, encountered and had sex with someone of that rare race? She could have easily ended the pregnancy, of course. It was in the middle of her medical studies and not at all convenient, but ending it had not entered her mind. She had been careful about birth control, so it had puzzled her. But Seiti had been a gift from the moment her tiny zygote took up residence in her.

The many eyes of their audience made Yanda uneasy. "What are we doing here?" she asked.

"We would have, of course, brought you sooner, but it was easier to...well, Melcraf finally had exactly what she needed."

What could that have been? Seiti? "Does the smoke creature control you?" Yanda asked, looking from one parent to the other. "Control Melcraf?"

Dal'an barked a strange, strangled sound. "You have much to learn, daughter. You know nothing of the history—"

Heat ran into Yanda's face. "How would I know, Mother? You deserted me as an infant." Her breaths came quick and shallow. Not easily assimilating the strange atmosphere, she lost consciousness.

Yanda woke in a small chamber of rounded walls, reminding her of stories of ancient dwellings carved out of mountains. For a brief moment, she panicked again, finding no oxygen, but remembered to carefully monitor her intake of the smoky air. If it could be called air.

Her mother sat stiff-backed beside the bed. "You have to learn to control your emotions," was all the cool female Xentu said in greeting.

Yanda considered the many things she could snap at her:

the many years without training, the utter lack of communication that might have given her a sense of who she was, the why. But she held back. "How long do you plan to keep me here?" she asked instead.

"As long as it takes to get you to bring us and Melcraf into orbit around Terlond," Dal'an said with no emotion. She ran her hands over her lap as though to press out invisible wrinkles.

"Why do you need to bring a whole moon? Why not just go live somewhere in the habitable universe?" Yanda coughed. Speaking made her jerk breath in too sharply, but she did not want to go into her mother's mind. She had no trust of this being who apparently had birthed her.

Dal'an's eyes flashed a lightning gleam, like a warning. "Moon. You think Melcraf is a mere moon? Just *any* moon?"

"What is she to you?" Yanda asked.

"You know her brother stones, do you not?" Dal'an asked. It was rhetorical.

"I do."

"And are they common?"

"You sound like you worship Melcraf. I have great respect for Shalt and Ash-don. I do not worship them." Yanda chose her words carefully, as though she picked her way across a mine field.

"What is worship? Do you worship yourself? You should. You are Xentu. But you have mostly wasted the abilities bestowed on you." Dal'an's features pinched as from a bad smell.

Yanda gazed at the tall, proud form next to the bed, hating her more and more. "I don't think I can last here all that long," Yanda said, feeling nauseous.

"You'll get used to it. Already you're adjusting. I can

see it. Using the Neyla transformation ability. Crude but sometimes effective." Dal'an's disdainful near-smile held a terrible beauty.

Yanda wondered if her mother ever smiled broadly, laughed with pleasure.

"But then, the sooner you bring us into Known Space, the better for you, for all of us," her mother added and Yanda saw that even allowing her to suffer was a planned game move.

Yanda heard threat in these words. Anger built, along with fear. She did not like her mother.

A familiar spark began in her belly. Ilan's presence tingled like sweet effervescence as his mind moved up through her to her brain. AI, Qontaqi skills, whatever it was, that was all he and the others needed.

Dal'an's face went from stormy and confident to enraged just as Yanda found herself on the bunker floor, on Terlond, Seiti beside her. Yanda pulled her daughter into a hug.

Yanda perceived a great mind-meld hug that squeezed her with affection. Shouma, Decru and Merne stood in a circle around them. Behind them, Ilan sat, Zami on his lap. She gave him a tremulous smile through a sheen of tears.

Zamani and Vatu walked toward them.

Tlalit got up from her elaborate computer chair. "I'm starved. I heard the dinner bells a minute ago."

Yanda pushed to standing, pulling Seiti with her. She bent to kiss Zami, whose arms wrapped around her neck. She lifted him, but not before squeezing Ilan's leg in gratitude. Melcraf and the Xentu intended to close her and Seiti off from outside help. But Ilan had found her across all Known Space and into the Unknown Universe.

"Yes. Dinner." But it was more fresh air and the feel of the land, the forest, the trees, that drew Yanda running toward the stairs, her boy in her arms. He laughed, and when they reached the bottom step, she glanced around for Seiti and saw her talking with Ilan. Zami lifted them both sailing upward toward the exit.

Outside, on the forest path, Yanda drank in the sweet Rotoulian air, filled with the scent of blossoms and utterly free of black smoke. Why would the Xentu stay on Melcraf breathing that black smoke? They could be anywhere. Surely with their powers they could make a place in the Known Universe safe for the Xentu race. She had again returned without answers. But she was so grateful to have been pulled back. She hugged Zami to her, as the others poured out of the bunker. As a group, they walked toward the elves' dining area. Zami scrambled out of her arms and trotted toward Merne who had Tuk-Tuk on her shoulder.

Just as they reached the long tables, thunder clapped and rain poured down. Tent canvases dropped from the trees and spread out over them. Glow-lamps brightened the spaces.

Yanda smelled rich gravies and yeasty baked breads and realized they hadn't eaten since the café that morning in Sheffed. A rumble in her stomach echoed the skies.

Vatu slipped an arm in hers and grinned up. "I love storms."

"Me, too." Yanda gave her friend a side hug.

She searched around for Seiti. The girl walked next to Ilan, both deep in animated conversation. Yanda experienced a tiny twinge of hurt that her daughter hadn't sought her out after their ordeal. Had she seemed too enveloped with Zami?

Vatu pulled her toward a table where Shouma and Chela were already sitting. Soon nearly all the ten fems were gathered around them. Conversation about their visit to Dondar swept her in.

Zami sat at the next table where several children of the Neyna had grouped, holding Tuk-Tuk in turns, chattering eagerly, punctuated by peals of laughter.

Yanda, with surprise, noticed Seiti across from the younger children, talking to an elf girl close to her age. Tentative hope played in her heart to see them interacting. She was unsure if the elf girl knew Universal or Seiti had a gift for picking up languages. Maybe even an implanted app. She'd ask tonight when they were back at their treehouse.

Shouma was telling the others how the Citadel had become a school. Yanda joined in as they conjectured about the interior.

"I wonder if the room we lived in is a classroom now," Chela speculated, before nibbling a nut wafer coated in truffle cheese. "Were you able to see in, Yanda?"

"We passed by too fast to take in those details," Yanda said with mouth half-full of mushroom tart.

"Is it a residential school?" Vatu asked Merne, who always knew those kinds of details with her miniscule screens everywhere. "I bet the servants' quarters are dorms now."

"I wonder what's become of our garden," Bonden said, tearing flat bread. Always serious, she carried a somber expression ever since her brutal captivity on her home planet of Qontaq.

Ilan, next to her, cast concerned eyes over his fellow Qontaqian, seeming to have the same thought about her mood.

"Would anyone want to get in there and look around?" Vatu asked. "I would, kind of." She dolloped a spoonful of crimson sweet jellies onto her sauteed *takla deets*.

Yanda imagined walking down those halls where fear had abounded at every turn. She still kept breathing in the air, willing Ilan and Decru to know that she didn't want to be pulled away to Melcraf like that again.

At the thought, Shalt rumbled. "I let you down." The Stone's unhappiness at its failure to keep her safe oozed in calamitous vibrations.

The diners stopped speaking and looked around.

Zamani, at the head of the table, stood and said, "Let's hold hands for a moment." A mind-meld with all the community was not common outside of Withum. "Shalt would speak."

Remaining seated, they clasped each other's hands.

Shalt's voice reverberated through them all. "Sister Melcraf and the Xentu did something unthinkable today, stealing Yanda, and Seiti, who were under our protection, to Unknown Space, not just in spirit but in body, and threatening to keep them there unless Yanda draws Melcraf to orbit here."

Shalt and Ash-don never spoke against their sister. Eyes met around the tables, surprised.

Tears welled as Yanda caught Seiti's gaze. Yanda saw a storm of emotions battling on Seiti's face: guilt, contrition, and something else. Defiance?

Shalt went on. "I will confer with Ash-don. Maybe it isn't the time yet for this reunion. Melcraf is not as she was in the past, before our connection was sundered. The Xentu need a place but we must examine the possibilities."

A blast of lightning struck the skies.

"Circle of Vashal, we must tighten the dome again to bring maximum protection," Shalt said. "We will shorten shifts to keep your energy, as in the past during clear threat."

Zamani nodded. "I am sorry for this. And that I did not foresee it." With these words, he looked directly at Yanda, then at Seiti.

Yanda wondered if she should stand and say something. "It's not your fault," "I don't blame you," or "No harm done."

But Zamani bowed and walked toward her. She stood and climbed over the bench to meet him. Others began clearing dishes and leaving.

Zamani took her in his arms, her head at his sternum. "Those were terrible moments when I couldn't find your mind." He lifted her chin to study her face. "Did you suffer there in Unknown Space? You seem a little strained but otherwise…fine?"

"I suffered a little," Yanda conceded. "It was uncomfortable but I'm fine. Unless that dark smoke does something to us. What do we know about it? We pulled something like it from Bonden."

"I think it's the same. We've studied that sample."

"When Merne took it away? She was bringing it here?"

Zamani nodded. "We have an extensive lab on the lowest level of the refuge. Vatu wants the Mingalian scientists to examine it, and of course the Neyla want some."

"Maybe they can extract some from me," Yanda said, mouth pressed in a wry smile, hoping there was nothing to extract.

"That would be wise," Zamani said. "You must be tired. Can I walk you home?"

Home, Yanda thought. Was her treehouse home?

CHAPTER

18

After dinner, Yanda read a bedtime story to the kids. They were all together in her loft bed. Any conversation with Seiti would have to wait. Yanda was exhausted; surely Seiti was as well, after the day they'd had.

The kids snuggled next to Yanda as she read about two Tellotian children.

"Like Gisli" Zami piped up.

"Yes!" Yanda said, holding the plaz reader, with its intricate illustrations, between them. "Exactly like."

Seiti studied the pictures, then pressed a finger to the screen of her ENAC 420. Text appeared as if her thoughts conveyed onto the screen. Well obviously, they did.

Three times as Yanda read, she was interrupted by mental messaging: Decru, and later Shouma, assuring her they'd monitor Seiti in shifts throughout the night. Zamani had also tapped into her mind and outlined the new protections instituted on Vashal.

As the children's eyes drooped, and the story came to a close, she shut the book. She thought she'd drop into instant sleep but for a long time she lay pressed between them, glad her daughter had stayed. Afraid to jostle their slumber, unable to settle her mind, she finally extricated herself carefully from the bed and climbed down the ladder.

Pacing between the treehouse levels, she ended up on a balcony, gazing at stars that appeared through shifting leafy branches. After a time, she tiptoed to the edge of the beaded curtain that covered Ilan's doorway, listening for sounds that he was still awake. She peered past dangling crystal strings and saw his form prostrate under covers in bed, glow-globes extinguished.

She was about to turn away when he said, "Come on. You're welcome to enter." He sounded amused.

She padded across the mats in the dark and scooted onto the bed.

He turned over to face her. "What's on your mind?" he asked, letting the darkness stay.

Sometimes it was good to talk with voices, not share from within another's mind. "I was thinking about home."

"You're longing for your childhood home?" he asked.

"Never that. No, I was pondering…Zamani called this treehouse home. 'Do you want me to accompany you home,' he asked. I've resisted thinking of Rotoul as a possible home."

"Why do you think that is?" Ilan asked, cradling his face in his hand, attention on her.

"I've wondered about that. I haven't had a home of my own, one of my design and choice, since my apartment in Skarth. Now it's a rebel headquarters." She shrugged, letting out an awkward laugh. "Not that I mind that much. Maybe I don't want to be there either."

"What was your home like, growing up?" He flung covers over her as she shivered in her thin night shirt.

She snuggled down into a pillow, her face level with his. "I liked the fields outside town the best."

"What did you like about them?" he asked, his voice low and soothing.

"My friends and I could make forts in the low bushes, and we always found tunnels. They never knew I could see them from above the ground. Thought I just had a sense. Called me 'mole girl'." Seeing his brows raise, she grinned. "Not in a mean way. I suspect they had gifts as well but back then...we were afraid to expose that. Always told that could lead to...trouble." She'd not given those years much thought recently. "I don't think I'd want to live there again. But I have no idea where I might make a future." Why was she telling him this? She shifted to lie on her back and stare up. Treehouses are never fully enclosed. A night owl coasted by. A setting moon jeweled the night sky. "Now I find I'm tied to the very people who deserted me. And because they're—we're—" she angled her gaze at him— "a special race that's been in hiding, I feel obliged to help them." She steepled her fingers in front of her face, then pressed them to her forehead. "I don't even think I like them." She curled toward him and waited for his response.

He reached out and ran the back of a finger down the side of her face. "You don't owe them," he said, affection and concern in his tone.

She shook her head. "I seem to carry a weight of obligation. The Stones want their third moon, their sister. Everyone says 'Xentu, whoa,' like worship. I sense accusation, like 'why don't you know this is important?' Why are they important? Will they help us free Blaz? Take down the corrupt Sinisay, and your *Senden Gares*? Kridenit? All the abductors? Tiklet? I don't even think—"

"You haven't had a chance to talk to your parents about their politics, have you?" Ilan said, reasonably. "What about Shalt, and Ash-don? Do you think they want their sister moon in orbit with them for a particular reason?"

"Shalt told me something, like they'd be amazing together, something the universe needs," Yanda conceded. "Do you think they might be a force for good, if they were brought together?"

"Maybe you should talk to Shalt again. We don't know if the Stones might even guide the Xentu folk toward bettering things."

Yanda gazed at him, studying his eyes, looking for hope. Then she shrugged a fraction, turned her face again toward the mats above them. "I got such a cold, unfeeling sense from my mom. How could they be good and give off that kind of icy…" Her voice dwindled away. She hadn't yet processed her deep disappointment at finally meeting her parents and encountering no joy in the reunion.

"They're desperate. They seem to need you and the Stones to help them," Ilan said. "Or to believe they can."

Yanda pushed up on one elbow. "Why though? Why does this have to be the solution? Bringing a whole moon—"

"We don't know. There seems to be more to it than just a moon." He gazed at her, hand under his face on the pillow.

"Dal'an said something like that. Like 'Do you think Melcraf is just any moon?' I wasn't feeling very good, and said, 'Yeah these stones are special. But I don't worship them.'"

"You know there's more to find out. But it's hurtful to you. I know it is." He laid his palm on her cheek and his thumb brushed a tear she hadn't known had fallen.

She sniffed and rubbed her eyes, starting to turn away but he pulled her into a kiss. She melted, resisting no longer. They'd held back, fought any temptation to become close. Their minds had already tasted the volatile nature of their connection. Could they handle love making?

Yet because of all the time—the trials they'd gone through together, the fondness built up as, time after time, they saved each other—had kindled fire. As they kissed— a burning kiss that lingered and grew—they explored each other. Clothes came off and at last he entered her. When he did, every cell ignited, sensations she welcomed, a wholeness of body, mind and spirit. She drew him closer, with arms, legs, every way she could bring him to her.

He shuddered and, holding her gaze, climbed into her mind, letting her fully into his.

Memories shot into her in flashes, him as a boy, his first love, heartaches, a crashing blow as his mind powers were too much for lovers.

These landed in her psyche but in no way interfered with her mounting orgasm. He formed a privacy sphere about them. As she came, she knew their moans and shouts were just for them, in their snow-globe.

Sweet tremors ran through her, lasting long moments. She wasn't sure it had ever felt like this. She smiled against his lips, giving him the snow-globe picture from her mind.

Grinning, he shifted their snow-globe to arrive in the midst of the crowd on Prokit's Moon. No one could see them as they watched the performance, the dancers and acrobats. They laughed, tangled together, warm flesh touching, still enflamed.

Yanda nestled her head into his shoulder, cheek to the dip of skin next to his collar bone. She kissed it.

Sometime in the night, Yanda awoke to find her back to Ilan, his heavy arm over her. His heft felt good, secure, substantial. She lay thinking about their lovemaking. She'd feared it would be too much, would even hurt their friendship. But it had been natural, full and right.

She'd have liked to languish there in his embrace, staying with the heated memories, but she needed to check on her kids. Carefully she lifted his arm and, with a sigh, slid out from under. She grabbed her nightgown on the way on the way out of the room. Deciding on a quick shower before snuggling with her kids, she snatched a towel from hanging shelves and stepped out onto the balcony where an outdoor shower could be concealed with a wrap-around curtain.

Once lathered with sweet scented soaps, rinsed and dried, she pulled her nightgown back on. In her quarters, she found Seiti on her own bed below the loft, a tiny glow-globe casting light on the pages of her notebook.

"Can I scootch in next to you?" Yanda asked.

"Sure." Seiti made room.

They sat side by side, pillows piled against the wide tree trunk at the head of the bed.

Yanda sorted through conversation starters and finally said, "It was quite a day."

"Yeah." Seiti's face seemed to grow strained, as though she braced herself.

"What is it?" Yanda whispered, turning on her side to look at her daughter.

"I don't know." Seiti's voice was barely audible and she shifted her head away.

Yanda barely breathed. "Is it...what Decru sensed in the van, that you have something you feel you have to hide?"

Seiti shook her head but then turned back to her mother and whispered in her ear as though others might be listening, "I was in a simulation, supposed to find something. I broke through to where I wasn't supposed to be. I loaded information into...I can't explain..." She paused. "It's a locked place in my mind. I don't know if they can find it, track it to me."

"You must have hidden it very well if Decru, Shouma, Gisli, no one detected it." Yanda tried to speak calmly but her dread roiled in her stomach. "Do you know what it is consciously though?"

"I don't dare. I have to keep it locked."

"Have you been aware of this all along?" Yanda hated to think that was the case. She guessed her daughter had seemed guarded, careful. It was so hard to tell after their time apart and all they'd both been through. A lot of times Seiti's expressions seemed a little too neutral, but Yanda put that down to the hardship of finding herself in a strange land, at a hostile school with sinister plans for her. Could this information she hid be what drew the Blaz fighters in the first place? At least that would remove suspicion that her daughter was a spy for the Tiklet school.

"I've known ever since it happened," Seiti was saying. "I was still at the school a long time after that."

"And no one ever mentioned it?"

Seiti shook her head.

"So maybe they *can't* detect it." After a pause, Yanda asked, "Are you sure it's still there?"

"Yes. I know it."

Yanda's heart raced but she said simply, "We'll figure something out, sweetie. Let's try to get some sleep. You want to stay down here, or come up with me and Zami?"

"I'll stay," Seiti said and turned back to her notes.

Yanda kissed her daughter's cheek. "Don't stay up too long drawing." She glanced at the pages lying open. She could not make out what was there. It seemed like rows of symbols completely unfamiliar to her. A code?

As she climbed the ladder to the loft, she mulled this over. The figures on the pages troubled her somehow.

Gisli burst into her mind. "Sorry. So sorry to intrude," the unassuming young man sputtered, "but something…you just looked at something that's set off snares we set under Dondar."

Yanda stopped mid-rung. "What?" She breathed out the word. How could he possibly have caught that picture in her mind? Had she broadcast it? "Have I—? Have we caused—"

"No. I think it's good. It might be a breakthrough. There's tight encrypting. We have it in an enclosed circuit."

Merne was already in the bedroom gathering Seiti, wrapping her in her blanket. Vatu emerged from her alcove, sleepy eyed, and hugged Yanda before they traded places on the ladder. Yanda paused to watch Vatu climb to Zami but was whisked instantly to the bunker.

They were in a garden room off the main IT level of the bunker. Multi-colored glow-globes lit paths of plants outside clear plaz windows. Soon abundant lounging furniture was filled with all the allies, Chela, Bonden, even Dele looking more rumpled than usual.

Yanda dropped to her knees by Seiti on a low settee as Gisli rushed in from the long underground hall. He knelt next to Yanda and, with no preamble, pressed his forehead to Seiti's.

The two of them had an easy relationship. Seiti put a trusting hand on the Tellotian's thin arm as he searched to help her unlock the mental repository. Yanda saw Ilan through the wall in the main IT center, already ensconced at the computer banks next to Tlalit, their faces reflecting the eerie blue from the monitors.

Ilan sent her a mental reassurance. "We're going to do this carefully. Don't worry." He gave her a swift, warm acknowledgment of their recent intimacy.

Despite the reassurances, she detected excitement in him and Tlalit, especially in Gisli.

Beri joined them in the garden room, gulping hot *kaffe*, making her long for some. Tenali followed. Vatu's slim childlike form ghosted through the doorway, a blanketed Zami in her arms, and settled on a wide chaise lounge close by.

Yanda heaved a happy sigh when several elves entered carrying baskets and trays that sent sweet yeasty aromas into the air. She lifted a warm roll and steaming cup from one of the trays and drank.

At last, Gisli pulled back and gave Seiti a hug. They spoke in soft voices.

Seiti lay against the cushions, curling into her blanket. She did not seem upset, maybe she even appeared relieved.

Gisli lay a hand on Yanda's shoulder. "It's good. This is very good. I don't think she knew she drew those symbols. It was maybe unconscious but it was the first wave in acknowledging what she was carrying around."

"Are they a code?" Yanda asked.

"Part of a coding language, yes. Incredibly classified. We've taken her notebook. I hope that's okay. I mean, I told Seiti."

Yanda nodded. "Of course." She patted her daughter's ankle reassuringly.

Zamani was one of the last to arrive. "I was on Vashal. We have a specific shielding for this latest work, to have extra protection in that part of our minds. I'm going to invite a full mind-share."

Yanda asked, "You trust absolutely every elf in Rotoul? Every guest? Every—?"

Zamani answered, in a low voice, "No I don't. That's why this particular shield gives a warning to all of us if any of the information is shared out of this community, if anyone even thinks about it."

"That's tricky," Yanda said, admiring the elf leader's poise in the midst of trouble. She found a pillow to sit on and set it near Seiti.

She'd thought Zami was asleep on the couch closest to them, but he suddenly got to his knees and proclaimed in some unknown language: *"Tadi ma grawn sa veyo…"*

CHAPTER

19

S eiti sat forward, staring at him. "That's the…that's what I was writing."

"It's a language, then. Not coding." Yanda gazed from son to daughter.

Decru appeared in the doorway and walked forward, holding the object he'd obtained the previous morning from the small part-elf he called Bleens. It shone, a dark blue cast.

"This is petrified *jaja* dung. From a large bird, nearly extinct, that nests in sea caves. It amplifies the unknown," Decru stated ceremoniously.

Gisli had been about to join Ilan and Tlalit inside. With an odd expression, he approached Decru instead and touched the dark stone with a fingertip. The air crackled.

Zami walked toward them, as if drawn. Decru sat, pulling Zami into his lap, and everyone else settled in concentric rings around him.

Seiti and Yanda sat on either side of Decru, then Gisli

and Vatu as the central circle. The others surrounded them, those with long legs—Ilan, Tlalit and other elves, Chin and the Jejods, in the third, back row.

The ancient *jaja* stone sent waves of energy through them all.

Zamani, next to Merne at the back, began the mind-meld. The garden room, which had been growing lighter from the dawn hour, became suddenly so dark that glow-globes, tucked into the vine-covered walls, lit up.

In the suffused light, pressed in among living, breathing bodies, Yanda felt cocooned.

Soon the powerful energy of the elven circles and Great Stones vibrated through her. Held by pressed-in shoulders, she watched as Zami, from Decru's lap, spoke in the other language, seeming to proclaim, as the oracle of the gathering. There was no need to translate. The hive-mind channeled the meanings.

Tear tracks glistened on Gisli's plum-brown face. "This was the language of a race on Tellot we thought died off." His voice cracked. He cleared his throat and went on, hoarsely, "Decimated by disease. Or stolen away to Blaz. There were rumors when they began disappearing but no bodies were found."

Yanda reached past Seiti to touch Gisli's knee. "That's so terrible," she whispered, eyes conveying her sorrow for him and his people. Then she asked, "Do you think the symbols in Seiti's book are their written language?"

"I believe so. I think Zami is speaking from the symbols in the book."

"And the meaning?" Tlalit asked from the back.

They all knew from ship life that she had acute hearing. Or some amplifying ability.

Eyes turned toward Gisli.

"No one's spoken the language for a hundred years. But I have a sense." Gisli looked at Zami.

Others followed his gaze. The little boy, with so many waiting to hear his answer, stood up to whisper in Decru's ear.

"Trouble," Decru said. "I think we all get that sense. Danger, fear, distress, loss."

"But no details," Zamani asked. "No information about what was happening?"

Vatu seldom spoke up to the larger group. Now she ventured, "We could put it through our language databases on Mingal. We've collected a lot of extant ones."

Seiti turned to her mother and quietly said, "There was a girl at Tiklet who reminded me of Gisli. We didn't see her often."

Low talking had begun around the circles but hushed. Someone in the back row murmured, "What'd she say?" A few in the middle row repeated her words.

Seiti went on, still too shy to speak loudly, "I think she may have drawn those symbols but she kept it pretty hidden. I caught glimpses." Seiti ducked her head, sensing the possible importance of her words.

"Telegraphic memory," Ilan said. "Maybe trained in. Vatu, let's connect with your Mingalian researchers and request translation."

"Okay." The bases of Vatu's head nubs turned rosy with the mix of pleasure and nervousness all the attention produced.

Yanda nudged her and gave her an encouraging smile.

"Break for a proper breakfast?" Merne asked. She seemed to be the food ambassador of the community.

As they stood, brushing off dirt and bark, Decru touched Yanda's arm. "Let's take our meal in the caves. I sense Shalt is anxious to communicate with you more privately."

Yanda hesitated. "Sure."

Decru turned to Gisli, Seiti, and Vatu. "Would you join us in my chambers in an hour? The waters in my pool might help us get some answers."

Zami, in Decru's arms, held the petrified *jaja* stone. He seemed at ease with it, also becoming very attached to it.

Yanda caught his eye. She thought, into his mind, "How does that blue stone feel?"

"I like it. It's a good object." He gave her a small smile.

"Not too much?" she asked, trusting that he could judge.

He shook his head. "Not too much. For me."

Inside, Yanda chuckled at his unassuming confidence. Then she felt Zamani gazing their way. She hoped he'd let them do this without him. Why? She'd never had an overbearing father. Kind enough, Nedri had been too checked out to dominate.

She resisted the urge to pull from Decru's grip on her arm, but protested gently, "I think I'd like to stay." Everything was just coming together, answers appeared to be emerging.

"You won't miss anything." He steered her ahead of him into the dark hallway of many screens, some dark, many lit up.

They climbed the stairs and then he took her and Zami by instant travel into his caverns deep in the labyrinth behind Shalt.

Decru led them to a table with dishes kept warmed by

large domed covers with elaborate handles in the shapes of creatures. Zami delighted in them and reached but Yanda held him back, not knowing how hot they were.

Decru lifted them with gloves to show a variety of steaming dishes, one with brown gravy. Another had red sauce. Cut up fruits bowls and bowls of nuts sat to the sides.

Yanda didn't know why they needed an hour, but when it was up, Vatu, Seiti, and Gisli walked in.

Steam obscured the faces around the dark water. Yanda let her mind slide into the meld that held the six. This time, Zami and Seiti and Gisli joined her, Decru, and Vatu in the dark pool.

When the *jaja* stone touched the water, alchemy shifted it to aquamarine and then to a troubling dark red. Bubbles tickled along her skin, then the waters roiled, churning deep below them. She held Zami tight on her lap, scooted back against the cave wall.

Decru, between Gisli and Seiti, asked Yanda's daughter, "Can you touch the stone without discomfort?"

Zami piped up, "I can." He wriggled as if to go to where Decru held the blue petrified object which looked like glass now, a light glowing through its many striations.

Decru gave the boy an affectionate smile. "Give your sister a little turn, okay, *japeet*?" He used a fond elven term.

Something happened then, inside Yanda. Faces formed on the walls and spoke to her. She tried to listen to both them and Decru but couldn't. What were they saying? Neither made sense. Maybe this *jaja* stone wasn't good for her. She sat more and more rigidly upright, distress mounting.

Shalt sent calming vibrations through her. "The *jaja*

glass will not harm you," the Great Stone intoned. It sent pictures into her mind, of a bird, prehistoric-seeming, human height, with long legs and large clawed feet that foraged on a forest floor. The bird flew to its nest in a cave by the sea. The walls below the shelved nests were layered in glowing vermillion excrement. "Let the bird glass into your heart. Let it be part of you."

The direction seemed vague but Decru was in her mind, guiding her toward the feeling, holding the stone's energy, emanating within her.

And then the surface of the pool became a scene— many scenes, one morphing into another, like a movie: violent abductions in the night, screams for help, buildings burning ...

When the water cleared at last, the six sat still, processing what they'd seen.

Zami had melted into Yanda, head resting to the side as if he might be sleeping. Seiti gripped her hands together in front of her staring at the waters and at Gisli. Vatu's nubs drooped along her scalp, as they did when she was overcome with sadness.

After a long moment, Yanda asked Decru, "Do the others know what we know now?"

"Soon," Decru said.

"Could some still be alive, on Blaz?" Yanda asked no one in particular.

"We can't know that from what we've seen," Decru said.

"But the girl at Tiklet..." Seiti said.

"What was her name?" asked Gisli.

"Oogleni," Seiti said. It was a whisper that swished around the walls of the subterranean cavern.

Gisli sat upright as if startled.

"What is it?" Seiti asked.

He shook his head and would say no more.

At the bunker, everyone agreed the afternoon needed to be for rest and relaxation.

Ilan left with the kids for the pools, Vatu right behind them.

"I'll catch up with you," Yanda said, needing a moment to herself. She sat on the edge of a balcony that skirted their bedroom, taking in shafts of sunlight. Soon, not wanting to miss time with her children, she gathered towels and a thermos and leapt off of the main landing to sail down through the forest, which was easy for her now.

As she glided over the bunker she spotted Beri pacing in front of Shalt's cave. She assumed he was trying to catch Decru coming or going. She knew he would never make it through the caves if he was not wanted there. Maybe he was prevented from entering. She slowed her descent, torn between the pools and her friend, when below her came a call, one she could never miss because his mind vibrations shivered in her heart and through her body. She glanced down to see Tenali come out of the bunker.

They'd spent so little time together. It would seem churlish if she kept avoiding him, or seeming to. She floated down to land lightly on the dirt path beside him.

He lifted his arms for an embrace but she stepped back.

"Oh, come on. We can't hug?" he asked, hurt in his eyes.

"Of course, we can." She relented, giving him a short hug, quickly pulling away.

"Can we talk?" he asked.

She hesitated, glancing toward the pools, then to Beri. She was sure Zami and Seiti were having fun with Ilan and Vatu. And Beri's attempts to talk to Decru were his affair, not hers. "Yes."

"On the hillside?" He gestured toward Vashal.

Where they had first stormily argued, where Tenali had first taught to float and soar, where they had talked in the forest, finding tender shared histories, shared wounds they'd never revealed to others. Should she go to such a memory-filled place with him now?

"Sure."

They climbed until the orange sun made them sweat. Wild herbs burst their seeds and slathered the air with pungent scents. Yanda waved an insect from her face and shoved errant curls back from clammy skin.

"How about half-shade?" Tenali asked, seeing the trickle down her copper skin. "Here?" He indicated soft tufts among far-spread saplings.

It reminded Yanda too much of their first intimacy. She perched on one grassy hump, ready to leave.

"You've been busy," he said, sitting on another.

"I have, yeah. My kids…"

"We belong together, you know."

She stared at him for a moment. "How do you work that out?"

His laugh was one sharp bark. "How do I not?"

"Well, let me see." She held a finger up as if to count off multiple reasons. "First off you kidnapped me for a rapist trafficker."

"We've been through that. We've been through so much since then." He'd scooted off his hillock and knelt closer to her, his face flushed. "Have I not proven my devotion since then?"

"Is that what you've been doing?" she asked. It wasn't a question. She leaned forward, elbows on knees. "Tenali, I've...Ilan and I are lovers." She sat up, thinking she must have landed a decisive blow.

But Tenali was not fazed. Not in the least. "We take lovers at times. A volatile life like ours is bound to...lead to that."

She raised her brows, wondering what he was confessing to. She realized what she was feeling was jealousy and berated herself.

He shoved his back to the other grass mound, facing her. "I don't care what you've done."

She laughed, out of disbelief more than humor. "What does that even mean? I'm not looking for forgiveness. I'm explaining something."

Tenali took a deep breath and heaved a sigh as if he prepared to enlighten a thick child. He said, nodding, as if to convey reason and wisdom, "I understand the big guy has solved some problems for you. Has even gone out of his way to display his powers—"

She started to protest.

He held up a hand to stop her. "—to help you. Granted." Sweat had soaked the dark curls near his face. His jade eyes crackled with emotion. He was ridiculously good looking in that moment.

Yanda did not need that right now.

"You've been through things that pulled you two together, made you close. Sacrificing to save Bonden. Saving Seiti."

"You helped, too," she said, thinking this wasn't a very strong argument.

"Yes, but not at your side. Not on the ship. He's had…access to you."

Yanda stared at him, not sure whether to laugh or be angry. "Access." She stood. "Look, it's been an intense morning and I want to go hang out with my kids."

"And Ilan."

"He's there, too, yeah."

"Can I come?" he asked, pushing to his feet. "It's only fair." He grinned, like he knew how irritating that was.

She shook her head. It wasn't worth quibbling over words. "I can't stop you. I mean it's a free—" she flapped her arms around her— "forest."

"Free." He fell into step with her, as they headed back down the hill. "What does the word mean? Are any of us free? Free from our pasts? Free from our worries, our choices, our—"

"Nope. Not really."

From where they were, they could see Beri, still outside the cave, squatting now by the opening.

"What's your pal doing?" Tenali asked.

"I don't know." Yanda pulled a brown leaf from a branch. "He wants to talk to Decru. You know he's a journalist."

"A snoop then."

"Basically. His sort of passion is power objects, and those who steal them from where they belong. That's how he gets himself into a lot of problems. And Decru is definitely an expert on objects with powers."

"True. But he doesn't think he can just walk in there, does he?" Tenali asked, jumping over a log.

"Probably why he's still outside." Yanda resisted snickering.

"Hoping he'll come out?" Tenali said. "I don't know the last time I saw the old elf come out that way. He has dozens of other paths to take. Most very hidden."

"Or just pops in and out," Yanda said.

Their feet touched down on a secluded stretch of path. Tenali held Yanda's arm. She glanced back at him. Sounds of playful activity at the water hole, punctuated by shouts and laughter, carried through a screen of trees.

She hesitated, taking in his appeal, leaning into it, then pulled away as conflictual loyalties wrangled inside her. "Come on," she said, and hurried toward her children, not daring to look again at Tenali, not trusting her own inclinations.

CHAPTER

20

Beri watched Yanda and Tenali coast on the wind. Against the sun, they looked beautiful, similar in ways. Both had two-toned hair and long curls, slender strong builds, and impressive poise. In comparison, Beri felt gangling and awkward. He glanced at his thin freckled arms covered in fine reddish gold hair and grimaced as they disappeared behind trees.

He'd been aware of Yanda floating down through the forest earlier and had hoped she might come to see him. In fact, he thought she'd noticed him and was changing course. But then she dropped out of sight. Tenali must have been the reason, he saw now.

Slowly he became aware of a venerable wisteria tree beside him, great bunches of purple blossoms weighing down its draping vines, the trunk rough and twisted, yet beautiful as the flowers. He knew it had to be in his mind, since nothing grew within a hundred feet of the entrance to Shalt's cave, the land still barren from the nuclear attacks decades before. Yet the flowering vine seemed part of the environment. He breathed in its gentle scent.

"What are you waiting for, outside Shalt's door," the tree seemed to ask him.

Beri crouched against the wall, edging away from the entrance which brought him closer to the vine.

"I know," the Decru-tree said. "You're a journalist. You need to investigate. You want *an inside scoop*." The old elf enunciated the last words, exaggerating.

Beri fancied he could see the elf's face, walnut hued, in the bark of the tree.

"But there's more," Decru went on. "A deeper reason than curiosity. I know what drives you."

Beri reviewed possibilities in his mind. What was the old elf referring to? Since he was quite often in trouble—though always with good purpose—he examined recent activities in his mind for anything he'd prefer the old elf didn't know.

"It's her," Decru said.

"Who?" Beri asked.

The leathery tree bark chuckled like a wayward wind and its long draping vines full of purple blooms rustled and swayed.

"Yanda, of course. Her worries are yours, more than any of your own."

Beri scraped his back down the wall to sit on the dirt, and studied his hands. "I'm nothing to her, though."

Why was he telling this leathery tree anything about his inner world? It did not seem like a choice. And he did want the elf elder to tell him things, in return.

"How do you know?" Decru asked. "I think she cares very much about you."

"I'm not at the center of her heart, though. Not like…" Beri didn't finish.

"Have you tried to be?" Decru asked. "When you were on Alland at the same time she was, did you make yourself known?"

How did the old guy know about that? Beri clenched his fists.

"She was alone," Decru said. "There was treachery. She didn't know who to trust. People stole her very home."

Beri's shoulders tightened. "But Ilan came along. He helped her."

"That might have been you. I know you *wanted* to help her. You *were* helping. In the end, your effort was crucial to getting her daughter back."

"You mean Gisli. I did nothing." Beri wiped dirt from his hands. Something was making him sweat all of a sudden. He rubbed his face and felt grit. The late afternoon sun against this wall had grown hotter. He shoved to his feet. "I think I'll go swim."

"I thought you wanted to interview me," Decru said.

Beri stopped, laughed a self-deprecating chuckle. "That is what I wanted," he admitted. "But you seem to have grilled me instead." He dropped a hip to the stone wall and studied the lush old vine. "Are you offering an interview?"

"I'm sure there'll be another chance, young yarn-spinner." The branches sawed and leaves rustled.

"I'm not sure I'd dare."

Beri turned and strode away across barren land toward the tree-line paths that led to cool pools, feeling laid bare and still chuckling to himself at how Decru had had the upper hand every inch of the way. As he walked, the whispering of invisible vines followed him, until the cave was long out of sight.

The sounds of splashing and shouting on the far side of a woody copse drifted to him.

Yanda stood, back to a sun-warmed stone, watching her children with Ilan, Vatu, and others, swimming, splashing, laughing. Tenali had come up behind her, in the shade of a river willow.

She longed to strip off her clothes and jump in with the rest. She'd turn *lanten* as she hit the water. Sometimes she didn't want to take that wild nature on board.

Glancing to her right she saw Merne contentedly crafting woven reeds. Children played in a nearby, shallow pool, teen elves with them.

Yanda pushed away from the rock and crossed to sit next to Merne.

"Hello." Merne shaded her eyes and looked Yanda over, then glanced behind her and smiled the warm loving greeting of a mother, especially one whose son had been gone very far away, too long.

Tenali threw himself on his side on the sand, head propped with one bent elbow.

Yanda glanced at him, then said quietly to Merne, "I want to learn more. When I go *lanten*, I want to keep my head, or be able to glamor that state from others' sight. I'd like to learn to travel instantly, like you, and disguise myself and others—"

Merne lifted a hand. "Stop." She chuckled. "I'm sure you're capable of all of it." She touched Yanda's arm. "I'm glad you're ready to go deeper with your skills. You'll be formidable someday, more than you already are."

"I want to learn, too," Tenali butted in. "I've never learned *lanten,* for instance. Do you think I can?"

Something brotherly stirred in Yanda as she caught Tenali's eye, imagining them learning together.

Emotions swirled deep in Merne's eyes. The corners of her mouth pressed down and wavered, as though she didn't trust herself to speak. She said into their minds, "This is a good moment. A greater commitment to your birthright, son." She stroked his wild, dark hair with affection, then brought her gaze back to Yanda. "And maybe a little softening toward Rotoul for you?"

"I'm soft toward Rotoul," Yanda defended, but she recognized that her reticence and protection of Zami must have been obvious.

"We can teach you all we know." Setting a complex cerulean weaving in her lap, Merne took Yanda's hand,. "But your family of birth will have…skills that are different. They may want to be the ones to teach you—"

Yanda snatched her hand back. "I'm not learning anything from that woman who calls herself my mother." Her lips were tight, teeth clenched. "They can keep their Xentu skills." She said the last words with venom, still aching from the recent disappointment of being pulled to Melcraf for such a cold reception. It seemed to her deception was her people's main skill.

"Very well. Decru seems to do well showing you internally what the skill is. Maybe we can work with you both." Merne took up her weaving project.

Ilan gazed at the beach where Yanda and Tenali talked with Merne. It worried him. Of course, he knew Yanda and Tenali had briefly been lovers. What bothered him now about this clustering? Did Tenali lean in toward Yanda too familiarly? It was more the quality of the air around them, he decided. A warmth rose from the pair as though it colored the air orange-red. And gold. A lot of gold.

The crazy, red-haired Romden journalist dashed past him and took a long flinging dive out into the middle of the pool. He was a sleek swimmer. You had to give him that.

Friendships, Ilan mumbled to himself. So what if Yanda had lots of male friends. She was inspiring, always with some exalted mission, never for herself, never for personal gain.

But after their intimacy last night, he'd thought everything would be different. Clearer. More solid.

"Mama," Zami called from nearby and paddled toward shore.

Yanda waded out fully clothed to meet him.

As the water line rose up Yanda's legs, she felt the beginnings of *lanten*.

"Let me help you." Decru was in her mind. "Find the core of it. Where did the magic begin?"

Yanda thought of those first moments, when Mnenu used his inimical method to ignite her transition. Her cheeks burned.

She pushed the thought away as she swept Zami up and around. He squealed. She pulled him into a hug and eased into a sidestroke toward deeper water. Zami pushed off to swim for Vatu who was sending bubbles out across the water.

"It doesn't have to be so..." In her head, Decru searched for the right word, then gave up. "Mnenu used a kind of shortcut."

Decru seemed a tad disapproving.

The wily old elf did have a way of gathering large swaths of her memories before she had time to tuck some away. She suspected it might be useless at this point to try to hide any.

"But now you must follow those sensations. Where do they emerge from? Swim away from the others and as *lanten* approaches, follow its development."

She *had* managed to slow the process, she realized, in order to greet her little boy. If I can slow it, I can stop it, she thought.

"You can. But you'll want to have every form of control," Decru told her.

"Yes, I do want that, and much more," Yanda conceded.

"Merne just told me."

"Admit it. You were eavesdropping." Yanda grinned.

"Maybe just a little." The old elf sat at his desk, the surface covered in myriad intriguing objects. "I had a conversation with your friend Beri."

"Oh, yeah, I saw him by the cave entry. So you granted him an audience?" Yanda asked, enjoying the royal sound of that and thinking it fitting.

If elves had kings, either he or Zamani would be one. Perhaps Decru the king and Zamani the advisor.

"Of sorts. It was a first assessment. I wanted to let the young scallywag know it won't all be on his terms."

"I'm sure you got that across very well." Yanda swam languidly away from the others.

"I believe I did."

Yanda found herself making her way to the tunnel that led through to a secondary pool, in a small grotto.

"That's good if you want to practice now," Decru said to her.

"Maybe briefly. I do want to get back to Zami and Seiti. I haven't had a lot of time…" Always, she felt pulled between. She didn't have work hours. How different it was from her life as a surgeon. Everything measured, scheduled. Would she ever live a life anything like that again? This way of living seemed to put her life on hold. How would her kids be educated? But why couldn't she see what they were doing as education? She scooted onto a rock shelf. "Okay. I'm ready."

Decru stepped from a cave opening behind the shelf where Yanda sat.

"Oh. In-person lesson. Lucky me." Yanda grinned up at him, tall and impressive, like an old tree.

CHAPTER

21

That night, Yanda finally had time with her kids. She'd turned down every invitation for the evening. She hadn't realized that what Decru would be teaching her would be so taxing. Yet also miraculous. Decru could become any creature. He could start out next to her and suddenly appear across the pool, or perched above her head, a *jaja* ready to take flight.

"Where are we going to live?" Seiti asked suddenly. She lay on her side on one of the couches in their tree-house's main sitting area, fingers swift over holographic keys that spoke to her ENAC.

"Good question," Yanda said, pushing up from drawing with Zami.

Ilan was a comfortable fixture in the largest chair which reclined at various angles.

"I think we'll have to figure that one out together," Yanda went on.

"Will we be in a school?" Seiti pursued.

Yanda thought about the incredible amount they could learn from the many talents surrounding them there. Of course, the other fems weren't likely to stay forever. "What if we sort of crafted a school here? I can't imagine anywhere with more abilities available to fulfill your potentials." She glanced at Ilan.

His eyes came up from his screen and he nodded. She couldn't tell what he thought, though. He was keeping that to himself.

"Where would you live if you could live anywhere, Mr.— Wait, I don't know your surname," she said to Ilan, bemused.

"Telfer."

"Ilan Telfer." She tasted that.

"What's yours?" Ilan asked.

She knew he knew hers. He had to. He and the other rebels had been all through her apartment and everything in it, including information in the walls that even she had no idea of.

"Dr. Yanda Artel. But that's my foster parents' name. I don't know my birth one. Our birth one." She looked at her two children in turn. Their eyes were on her, expectant. "Maybe you know, Seiti." She still hadn't learned all that had happened with Seiti on Melcraf. Yanda scooted her back against a settee. "How much time have you spent on Melcraf?"

Seiti glanced around at the others, then slid into sitting, pushing aside her ENAC. She swallowed. "I can't be certain. Sometimes I thought I was there and other times I thought I'd been dreaming. Maybe I was."

"What did you find out?" Yanda asked softly, not wanting to turn off the tap of sharing.

"Well, our name would have been Nandim."

"Do you know why they gave me away?" Yanda asked, her throat so tight it hurt to ask.

"They only planned for you to be fostered there. But then they couldn't return."

"Do you always believe what they say?" Yanda asked her daughter.

Seiti shrugged. "Our foster parents Omshi and Nedri betrayed them. They're banished. But—"

"Banished." Yanda repeated the word. "From what?"

Seiti shrugged. "Your foster parents—my Nana and Papi—betrayed them. They're banished. But—"

"Banished?" Yanda repeated the word. "From what?"

Seiti's lips turned up, sad, apologetic. "The Xentu."

"They're Xentu?" Yanda sat up straight. "But they hated our powers," she whispered, holding Seiti's gaze a long moment. They'd shared years of Omshi and Nedri's strangeness, rejection from foster parents and grandparents for who they were in their essence.

"I know. I don't really get it." Seiti picked up her ENAC and turned away enough that Yanda sensed retreat.

Yanda stood. "Anyone want herb tea? I think I'll fix something minty." In the small kitchen area, she waited for the water to heat. Here, she could actually draw on nature to hurry the process. She wondered if that would be the case now anywhere there were plants, things growing, or if the ones here in the elven forest were more willing. Ilan followed her. From behind, his broad hands warmed her shoulders. She turned into his arms as a single tear escaped and he folded her in a hug.

"It scares me," she whispered. "I want to know all but am also drained by it."

"It's a lot to take in." Ilan stroked her back.

In the sitting room, one step down from the kitchen, the children were quiet, Zami building a design into the air, a new skill he'd picked up among elf children. Seiti concentrated on her ENAC.

Yanda poured steaming water over leaves and brought cups and pot for everyone, on a tray with biscuits. Ilan followed with honey and cream from the milk plant.

Settling on the woven rug against the couch, she spooned honey into cups and set milky tea by Zami. "It's almost your fourth birthday. I don't know if I can call you Button anymore."

He turned to her and asked, quite seriously, "What will you call me then?"

She studied him. "Hmm…I don't know." She tapped her lip, pondering.

"Squibbish?" Seiti suggested. It was a particularly annoying bird of the Rotoulian forest that cried in a shrill voice over and over. She'd called him that several times even though he was never shrill.

Zami made a face at her and touched his cup tentatively.

"I can cool it with more milk," Yanda offered.

"I'll cool it." Zami got on his knees and hovered over the cup, looking intent. Then he touched it and smiled. "Perfect." He wrapped his small hands around it and drank.

"There's a Qontaqian marsupial called the *patat*," Ilan said. "I've been tempted to call you that."

"Why?" Zami asked, licking foam from his upper lip.

Yanda hadn't known Ilan was listening.

"Sometimes you have an expression a little like them." Ilan blew on his tea and sipped.

"I might call you both 'til a new name comes along. Do you have a preference?" Yanda asked her son, tasting her tea. It was a blend of mountain mint and other local plants. A lovely soothing scent rose to her in the steam.

They stayed on safe easy topics the rest of the evening but what Seiti had said haunted Yanda. Now she had to know the truth of her origin. She had a decision to make that could affect all the inhabitants of the universe.

By the next morning, Yanda knew she'd basked in the warmth and comfort of family as long as she could afford, and made her way alone toward Shalt's cave. The sun was high and intense as she crossed the stretch of barren land from the woods near the bunker to the cave opening. Stepping into the dark entrance, the temperature dropped sharply, a welcome coolness that quickly turned to frigid cold.

Shalt had been calling to her for days but she'd wanted to collect her own mind. So much kept happening, with more and more revealed. What Seiti had told her the night before threw off her entire sense of her childhood, and Seiti's. It was unfathomable that her foster parents had the same powers as her birth parents. She wasn't sure exactly what all those powers were except that everyone she met was impressed by them.

It was time to delve deep, get the whole story, and she surmised that Shalt knew it. She crossed to the thirty-foot hole and gazed down upon the glowing stone that seemed to stretch to eternity beneath the crust that held her.

For a moment she contemplated whether she should instead journey to Ash-don for the next installment of the story. She had no strong belief that anyone would impart the entire history to her; after all, they never had before. It came in dribs and drabs. But approaching Ash-don was a full experience of immersion in cold, roiling waters, then crawling in animal form onto the Great Stone's surface as she shifted to *lanten*.

Reaching Shalt could be just as organic, she told herself, just a different element—air. She made her decision and pushed off from the ledge, sweeping down toward Shalt's smooth opalescent mantel. Now used to the jolt of the stone's energy, she dropped to crossed legs. For several moments she breathed deep, taking in the Stone's powerful force that coursed through her. Then she stretched out, facedown. Pressing her forehead to the surface, she looked through layers with her mind. Moss agate patterns formed and changed in the interior.

She laid her cheek to the stone as their connection strengthened. "When you first called me...you knew I was Xentu. You knew the history of my people, my race, didn't you?" She felt a tear smudge on the stone under her face. She let the dampness stay.

"I know...many things." The Great stone's tone was not arrogant. It was sad. "I know I tore you from your daughter."

"We've covered that. I understand why you did it. But I'm not sure why you've left me with so little information when we've spent such intense time together. You gave me your history with Terlond in the blink of an eye. Why not the facts about my own race?" She traced a tear across the opaline surface, watching the rose glow that followed wherever she touched.

"It is a fair question. You may as well join us, Decru. I sense you listening in."

Decru appeared in his tailored clothing of rich colors and fine fabrics. He lay on his side as if the stone's surface were a settee in his living quarters. "You're troubled," Decru observed to Yanda. Distress did not show on his carved face but she felt it in his mind and heart.

She thought she wanted the dignified, clever elf there; they'd shared deeply in recent days. Yet he had a powerful presence that could hardly be called comforting. Shouma would have been more settling.

She rolled onto her back and stared into the blackness through the opening in the rock rim circling above.

Decru maneuvered so the crown of his head touched hers. Surprising warmth poured into her, settling jangled nerves, brightening dark places. She stretched out her arms, letting in heat from Shalt as well. It gentled into her bones.

"You're right that I'll never tell you everything. At least not all at once," Shalt said.

"Do you know everything?" she asked. "For instance, do you know what's happened to Gisli's people, stolen from Tellot?"

"I don't know everything. And some things are not mine to tell. Discovery is part of any conscious existence. Human, elf, Jejod, Stone. Sentient beings of every creed and hue." He paused and the vast stone shuddered with some mineral emotion she couldn't hope to identify.

"Okay, so you deemed that it was to my benefit, or at least my fate, to go into all I've been through knowing only a small part of the story you could have imparted to me. That was a decision on your part. You shaped that situation." She didn't usually speak with this kind of candor or harshness. Was it a change in her, or just coming to a particular place in their relationship? Who could say?

"I think you give me too much credit, Allandian. Do I reason through these things? Do I strategize with you and other beings like pieces on a chessboard?"

"I don't know. Do you?" Yanda asked. "Because the alternative is that you have no choice in what you do in my mind, what you express, what you share."

"Maybe I can help in this," Decru murmured. His mind register came across to Yanda as relaxed, yet keenly alert and inquisitive. "Shalt's qualities that connect with intelligent, sentient beings give life energy and attune to the survival of those he's attached to, including, maybe most of all, to the stones he holds dear. In that vein, he collects knowledge of what has occurred over time—millennia—but he does not always work with it in the ways we identify as human or elven thought."

"I think I get that. So, I should let Shalt off the hook regarding what I still don't know?" Yanda turned on her side, propping on one elbow to look at Decru.

"Ask me," Decru said, peering up at her.

"Oh, so I should blame you." Yanda's stomach shook with a building giggle. It seemed absurd to talk to either of these wise beings, old as the crystal in the pyramid above them, older in Shalt's case, of blame. Maybe her worries seemed small. Maybe they were as big as everyone's survival. Her smile dropped away. "Shalt called me Allandian. What was my original planet? Where was I born?"

"Let's settle comfortably and I'll tell you what I know," Decru said, closing his eyes.

Yanda lay back down, head-crown to his.

CHAPTER

22

The Xentu are a very old race," Decru began.

"Where did they begin?" Yanda asked. She didn't want to interrupt but didn't want to miss this single piece of information.

"No one knows. Myth has it they had their own world, with elaborate structures, amazing art and libraries, but there's no record of where it might have been."

"How can that be?" Yanda snapped.

This gap made the aching need to know seem trivial. But she decided to leave it for now. There were other essential questions.

"What are the Xentu skills?" she asked.

"They can build, seemingly out of nothing. They built the golden city."

"Here on Terlond? In the tunnels?" she asked.

"Yes. They left their world. No one knows if it was destroyed, or if they erased any sign of having been there. Maybe erased the knowledge."

"But why?"

"That's the bigger question. What we do know is some around the universe wanted to use their powers. Just like they came here for the Stones. For Shalt. Of course, greed must always come into it. They stayed a while here but then something almost worse happened. One or some among them became twisted. They had such a powerful mind-meld that one Xentu could harm the many. Rather than banish him, they left and hid."

Decru maneuvered around so he faced Yanda. "You were the last infant born to the Xentu. Omshi and Nedri took you away to Alland."

Anger bubbled in Yanda. Questions flew out of her mind as she learned of the reason she'd been alone all her life, often misunderstood, even treated as a pariah.

Decru seemed to search for words that would help. "I don't think they knew how to handle the dangerous aberration."

"So they ran and hid." Yanda grappled with the expectation of bringing Shalt and Ash-don's sister to them, along with the Lost Xentu people, those who had caused her the long isolation, abandonment, and rejection that had plagued her life.

Decru reached out and touched her arm. "The Xentu have watched you and Seiti as the last hope for their race. They are proud of you."

"Dal'an doesn't act proud of me. She just seems surprised by powers I haven't mastered." Yanda heard herself as childish in light of all they faced now.

"The dark smoke on Melcraf," Decru said, jolting Yanda with his shift in subject, "we believe is the essence of all powers."

Yanda sat up. "Did it originate with the Xentu? Did they bring it to Melcraf?".

"It may have started there," Decru said. Yanda thought he listened to the Stone for answers now.

Why did Shalt not tell her directly?

"Yanda, we think—I should say the Stones, but also the elves—believe we can heal the Xentu and prevent the dark one who emerged among them—"

"Where is he now?" she asked suddenly, possibilities crashing through her mind.

"We don't know if he still exists. He hasn't been seen or perceived since they left Terlond. It's difficult for Xentu to leave the mind-meld and survive on their own."

"Tell me about it." Yanda couldn't help sarcasm popping out.

"If the Xentu are brought into orbit here. If the great stones can be three again..." It was as though Decru mouthed Shalt's words.

"But Melcraf is...it's miserable, uninhabitable. Why haven't they just come on their own?"

"They would terraform Melcraf, here where it's possible, in Known Space. You would be..." Decru searched her eyes, "most important, essential even, to this happening." Decru's loyalty to Shalt and the Great Stone's needs was unshakable. So was his faith in the Xentu people, from their great deeds of the past, their purported goodness, as a legend of the planet.

Yanda flashed to her time as a surgeon. She could perceive how a being's body should be and how to build it back to that state. On Alland, it had been prohibited. She could not even consult with others regarding this urge, but she used it in small ways to repair veins and other tissues.

"We believe you could develop the reparation skills not only with the physical body but with the psyche and powers." It was Shalt who inserted his voice here. "I have seen it. You know my sight is not limited to linear time. But don't get me wrong. I don't see everything. And things can change." These last were said with a rumble, pleading and urgent, for her to understand and not blame if he were wrong.

"What was the terrible thing this bad Xentu did?" Yanda asked.

There was silence and Yanda had to wonder where Shalt drew the information from.

"It had to do with time," the Great Stone said. "Changing time. Lives were erased, loved ones never having existed, yet remembered."

"That's vile. What was his name?" Yanda asked.

"It was Frast," Shalt said. "But he goes by Jelat now."

Yanda's heart squeezed with a jolt that ran numbing wires down her limbs as her mind raced to the baby-faced tech wizard on Alland who'd betrayed her, misled the rebels, and was in the midst of everything: their information, their networks, their lives. She scrambled to her feet, calling to Ilan and Gisli with her mind as she shot away from Shalt's surface and into the cave above, abruptly breaking the connection with the Stone and Decru. At first she ran, but then she transported.

Others heard the mental cry. Before she reached the bunker, most were gathering. Zamani headed down the stairs to the first level ahead of her. Ilan soon followed. They ran to the second floor with its extensive bank of computers, where they found the fems, Gisli, Beri, Merne, Tlalit and others.

Yanda rushed to Ilan. "It's Jelat. Oh gods."

Shalt called to her, "We cannot fight this without the Xentu fully in their power. You need to think this through."

Shouma wrapped her arms around Yanda, who melted into the motherly embrace, breathing in the exotic scent of the Sonda's favorite incense, exuding from the elder's hair plaited in wrapped braids.

"You must tell us, child." Shouma pressed a hand to Yanda's chest. "Your heart is thundering."

"We have to stop him, now," Yanda said to Ilan over Shouma's shoulder.

"We've had our eye on Jelat. He does nothing we aren't aware of."

"Are you so sure? You don't know who he is. You don't know what he's capable of. Not really. Not the unthinkable that sent the Xentu into hiding." She moaned low in her throat with dread.

"What do you mean?" Ilan asked, bringing his eyes close to peer into hers.

All attention was on her as they waited to understand her shock.

"He's the one. He's the Xentu who drove them away." She explained the best she could. "He can manipulate time. Erase loved ones as if they never existed, but they did." When Yanda saw puzzlement on the others' faces, she tried again, "He changed the past. No one's past was safe from him."

She spotted Vatu holding Zami and pushed through to them, pulling her toddler into her arms, pressing her cheek to his. "We have to bring Melcraf here, and heal the Xentu. And seal off, I mean STOP him, from any thoughts, any actions at all!"

Shouma laid warm hands on Yanda's shoulders. "Slow down, *meshooli*. You can't keep on like this. You need rest. Where's Soni?" she asked Chela who stood close by, worried eyes on Yanda and the boy she'd cared for from birth through his first year. "We should get Yanda into a healing bath. She's pale and clammy."

"You don't understand. We have to act fast." Yanda shook with desperation. No one seemed to be doing anything.

"Jelat's active on the dark web right now," Gisli said from a computer station at the side of the long narrow room. Facing the screen, Yanda only saw his plum face lit up. "I think he senses what's been revealed."

"Cocoon him." Yanda turned wild eyes to Ilan. "AI? What can you use? Merne?" She searched for the elf leader's daughter. Spotting her she cried, "You have to go. Get him. Freeze him."

"Jelat is frozen," Tlalit said from the station next to Gisli's, her tangerine skin turned lavender by the screens.

"Should we bring him here, to our caves?" Merne asked, standing next to Tenali.

"Maybe better to watch his activities, see who's connected to him, influenced by him," Beri said. He'd maneuvered close to Yanda and now patted her shoulder reassuringly.

Ilan drove a hand into his thick rust hair which had grown longer recently so that curls stood up. His expression was dark and brooding. He'd worked with Jelat, had seen him as duplicitous, in bed with the enemy, but not this: Not the bitter foe of the Xentu community, an ancient appearing as the young, brilliant, well-intentioned rebel.

Ignoring Beri's comment, Merne and Tlalit jumped to

action, shifting clothes and appearance right in the hall, trying on dark flexible outfits, making themselves smaller, even turning into marsupials and primates, creatures that climb easily.

"This has to be planned carefully," Gisli urged, watching them.

"As intricately as saving Seiti," Beri agreed.

"What if I go along with them and distract him?" Seiti asked.

Yanda stared at her. "Why you? No. I don't want—"

"He wouldn't suspect a girl," she said.

Ilan pushed to standing. "You think not, Seiti? He can read your mind register." He stepped close to the girl, protective.

"Are you so sure?" Seiti had a determined look unlike any Yanda had seen on her before.

"We should bring Jelat here first," Yanda said, incredulous that there was any question.

She held Seiti's hand as if to make sure she went nowhere without her consent.

"Let's get him, then focus on pulling Melcraf across the universe," Tlalit said with her usual firm authority.

"Who should go?" Yanda asked the throng.

"Vatu, you're the slickest for transforming self and others. Will you join us?" Merne stood in the middle of the gathering.

Vatu nodded. "Of course."

"I'm coming." Decru stood to one side.

Yanda had not noticed him until now. She caught a glimpse of something translucent and round held in his hands.

The four—three elves and a Mingal—disappeared.

Moments later, Decru stood in their midst holding the small round crystal. Now a tiny figure squirmed inside.

"Is that Jelat?" Yanda asked, staring. She still gripped Seiti's hand. Relief washed over her, that her daughter hadn't been involved.

Merne nodded, disgust on her face as she indicated the translucent object in Decru's hands before he slipped it into a dark bag.

"I wanted to go," Seiti said. "To help." She bent to stare down into the bag, angry tears threatening to fall.

Yanda knelt to look into her daughter's eyes. Quietly, almost in a whisper, she asked, "Were you thinking you would use your child weapon training?" Her gut ached to say the words, and her throat squeezed painfully.

Seiti rested a hand on her mom's neck and gave her a brief glimpse of the past. It was enough. Jelat had been the one to send Seiti off Alland, to be captured by the Blaz.

Yanda sat back on her heels. Her stomach lurched. Bile rose. She longed to destroy what Decru held.

Shouma encouraged Yanda off her knees. "This part is done."

Elves came into the hall with snacks and brought them to the tables in the subterranean courtyard. Yanda tried to nibble a wafer with a faint toasted seaweed flavor but found her stomach too disturbed. She noticed Ilan, standing to the side, brooding.

His gaze came up to meet hers. "I didn't see it," he said into her mind. "I didn't protect your daughter." He studied Yanda's blanched face. "Come. You need to eat. Are you going to attempt bringing Melcraf tonight?"

"I have to," she said, though she longed for bed.

CHAPTER

23

Yanda's fingers tingled with the position she'd held long into the night, drawing Melcraf, small among moons but a large body to draw out of Unknown Space with its strange sticky dark matter, and across the Known Universe.

Tenali and Decru fanned out so the three formed a pinwheel on Shalt's surface. Having borne a piece of Shalt in his skull until Yanda removed it, Tenali had a growing connection with Shalt and was quickly becoming one of the Stone's greatest voices.

Above them, in the large domed cave, Shouma, Bonden, and the rest of the talents did their part in moving, guiding, and protecting Melcraf as the moon made its way to Terlond.

"Ready to jump her?" Merne asked into all their minds.

The Circles, and the many joined in the mind-meld, drew their energy into higher frequencies as they prepared to send Melcraf in hyper-speed leaps. Tlalit, Gisli, and Ilan had pinpointed intervals across the universe, to finally place the moon in orbit around Terlond. Shalt and Ash-don would provide the major power for the jumps.

Yanda gave herself over to the intensity of the Great Stones channeling through her. She did not understand it, but knew now how to be the conduit of the cry, the call that magnified and magnetized all their strengths. As though she were a mighty tree trunk, she opened to the blast that seemed ready to burst her heart, but never did.

And then they were all seeing the moon's approach through the vision of those looking directly at the sky with telescopes or on screens.

Melcraf took her place as a fourth moon circling Terlond. She would set, and rise, as did the blue Eshet, pale yellow-orange Salit, and soft green Talal.

"What do the other moons think of her?" Yanda wondered, exhausted, euphoric. Worries about the Xentu coming there would wait.

"I have never detected sentience from the other moons," Shalt responded, clearly glowing and tingling with satisfaction of having their sibling moon back with them.

Maybe Melcraf will wake something in the other moons, Yanda said in tired mind-speak. "Is Melcraf slightly pinkish here or is it my imagination?"

"We'll see what color she is once terraformed," Mnenu answered.

Yanda had known he must be in the Neyla circle helping, but hadn't sensed him separately until that moment. She greeted him personally across the miles of ocean between. The Neyla leader had studied various life-seeding, undersea and on land, at university and was clearly excited for this new project on Melcraf.

Yanda sensed Seiti calling to her, "Mom, are you coming up here with us?" She had joined those in the cave who drew Melcraf, and her grandparents.

"Yes." Yanda pushed away from Tenali and Decru. Knees cracking, she stood with a wobble.

"Good work tonight," Shalt said to her, "daughter." He sent vibrations up through her feet and legs to finish in her belly and heart, gentling the long effort they'd sustained. The stone glowed rosy where her weight pressed down, making her smile.

Tenali and Decru scrambled to standing as well. Arm-in-arm, the three rose to the ledge that jutted in a rough circle above, and glided onto the vast cavern's rock floor.

Seiti and Zami ran to wrap their arms around their mother. Yanda stroked their hair, holding them tight. She felt weak, an exhaustion that was not just weariness. A weight dragged on her. She longed for family time, and a hot bath.

When she looked up from her children, she realized the number gathered in the cavern had doubled. With trepidation, she saw that the space was half-filled with those austere faces she'd seen in the smoky room on Melcraf. The Xentu already mingled with her dear compatriots, the fems, elves, and other allies. A few elder elves embraced the Xentu, renewing old friendships.

So soon?

Then her birth mother stepped out from the crowd.

No, she wasn't ready. This was not who she wanted to see. She wanted comfort, a modicum of normality and calm.

Sensing her mood, Vatu and Shouma hurried over to Yanda.

Dal'an drew nearer and Yanda realized her fearsome birth mother was, in fact, no taller than her. On smoky Melcraf, she'd seemed to loom over her.

Dal'an hesitated. "May I embrace you?"

Yanda pressed her children's heads and shoulders closer, protective. But Dal'an stepped forward, hands out, palms up. Almost without volition, Yanda let go of Seiti and Zami and took her mother's hands.

Dal'an moved in close and slid her cool cheek against Yanda's.

Yanda stood rigid, longing to trust this woman who now seemed warm and affectionate, yet not trusting her at all. How easily Dal'an might withdraw the affection once Yanda accepted it, and it would hurt so much more if she'd softened toward her. She hated that Dal'an probably felt her shaking.

Dal'an pulled back and gazed into Yanda's eyes, hers now filled with tears. "You have found Frast and made us safe," she said.

"I didn't find him," Yanda countered. "Do your people feel safe now?"

"*Our* people, daughter. Yours, too, Yanda." Dal'an breathed deep of the earthy air. "We are at last able to be a community again, building, creating, taking part in the universe, or that is our hope. Our dream." She glanced at her husband and he nodded, his austere face attempting a smile toward Yanda.

"How will you avoid what happened before, Mother?" Yanda asked. "Will you race off to unlivable places when one of your kind again develops unpleasant skills?" She was surprised at the bold challenge, yet something was building in her. She felt Shalt and Decru bolstering her. She clung to Vatu, Shouma, and her children for strength. For a heart-stopping moment, she feared Seiti might side with the Xentu but all, including her daughter, willed her to know they were with her, and condoned her question.

Dal'an's eyes widened with the harshness and accusation, but rather than responding with anger, she turned a full circle, scanning those around them, Xentu and non-Xentu alike. "You draw good people to you, Yanda. The fems. The elves. Qontaqians and others. Even Mingal." She gestured to Vatu. "And Sonda." And she bowed slightly to Shouma.

"Ironically, it was Krid who brought the fems together," Yanda said.

"Yes. But maybe there was more at work," Dal'an said mysteriously.

"More at work?" Yanda drew up, eyes flashing. "Whatever you mean by it, I've had one Xentu secret too many." A storm brewed in her. She grew in size and rose off the ground as she had when they'd battled Krid. "You will not stay on this planet unless every one of you submits to Shouma's examination," she shouted. "I will have no more secret machinations. I do not know what you have been involved in, what parts of my family's hardships have been your workings from Melcraf, but believe me, I will know, and it will no longer be tolerated. That includes you, Tenali, who worked with Kridenit. I. Will. Know—ALL!"

She heard her voice thundering through the immense chamber that towered over them. A green-gold light saturated the air. She smelled it like a tinge of smoke after sparklers. The Xentu whirled toward the wall, pressed in a line against it, while her allies spun into a tight group around her.

Tenali was not in the allied group; neither was he with the Xentu but pressed into the crevices in the shadows at the back of the cave.

Risen off the ground, she could see over everyone's heads.

Out in the center, stood Decru, alone with his burden, his encapsulated prisoner. He bowed low to her.

"I will know everything," she repeated as she dropped back to the ground, striding toward the exit, her voice still carrying throughout the chamber. "The Xentu will not join us. Not yet." Children's hands in hers, Vatu and Shouma with them, they climbed the ramp and left the cave, allies following. She would let Decru and Scaton, the terrifying guard of Shalt's cave labyrinth, and anyone else needed to sequester the Xentu until their trial began, whatever shape that took. She sensed the Circle beginning a new vigil, communicating with Zamani. Much was afoot that she would entrust to others as she stepped out under the night sky.

She stared up at Melcraf, a rosy, three-quarter moon among the stars. The rest gazed up with her. Just then a thin dark cloud formed words in a trail across Melcraf's surface.

"What does it say on the moon, Mama?" Zami asked.

Seiti held up the devise she wore on her wrist. "I can find out."

Yanda laid a hand on her daughter's head, ruffling her hair. "Yes, please tell us." Then she said, low but still carrying to the allies standing around them, "Meanwhile, I'll celebrate a new moon and a growing, powerful community.

One of transparency. Without damaging secrets." She caught Ilan's eye and he nodded.

That wasn't enough but for now she would let it be. I will find a way, she thought. No one will lie to me, or hold back what I need to know. She thought about Arc and others she wanted to learn from. As they started toward the sound of the elven dinner bells, she moved up next to Merne, bringing Zami and Seiti with her. "That house you built by the sea. Near where the withum grows…?"

Merne said, "Yes?" curiosity puckering in a growing smile.

"Could I build something for myself and my children in that little valley?"

Merne let out a delighted laugh. "Yes. Yes, I can see that very well."

Several close by nodded, as though a growing dream stitched its thread between them.

THE END… for now.
The story continues in Book 5.

XENTU SECRET GLOSSARY

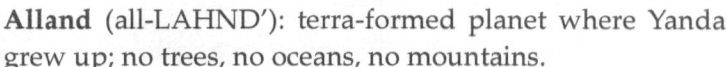

Alland (all-LAHND'): terra-formed planet where Yanda grew up; no trees, no oceans, no mountains.

Arc (ark): keeper of Pedore, man of strong mind powers; centuries-old. Protector of the crater, which is sacred to him and his kind.

Arsat (ar-SAHT): young Neyna elf, helps with kids.

Artel: last name Yanda carried as a child living with Omshi and Nedri, foster parents.

Ash-don (ASH-dawn): Power stone of the Neyla, Shalt's counterpart.

Balyou (BAL-you): the small town on Alland where Yanda grew up.

Bend: teen elf, helps with kids.

Beri ("berry"): captive of Krid, journalist from Romden; Yanda's friend.

blalims: bun made from mushroom flour.

Blaz ("blahz"): planet with terrible reputation: known for trafficking, violence, slavery.

Bleens: small part-elf man, friend of Decru, lives in a remote area at the north tip of Terlond's only continent.

Blenin (BLEH-nin): city on Shagal, where Seiti may have been spotted by Blaz traders.

Blue Mirrdoo (mer-DOO): café in Sheffed.

Bonden (BON-d'n): was one of the ten fems held in captivity by Krid; inventor, strong powers, can walk through walls.

Button: Yanda's nickname for her son, Zami.

Café Tellot (tell-LOT): in Sheffed near interplanetary mall; beach motif like tropical Tellot.

Chela (CHEH-lah): healer, fellow captive with Yanda.

Chin, Chinkendit (chin-KEN-dit): large soldier, mind powers, fem captive.

Church of Vital Promise: powerful single main church of Alland; has grown xenophobic; intimately tied with government.

Circle: a powerful circle that sits on high seats carved from mountain drawing energy from the Great Stones.

Citadel: Krid's mansion in Dondar; prison for fems with powers.

Dal'an (dahl-AHN): Yanda's Xentu (birth) mother.

Decru (deh-KROO): silver-haired Neyna elder; mainly occupies the underground labyrinth extending back from Shalt's caves.

Dele (DAY-lay): female Qontaqian, attractive, willowy, haughty; musician; fellow captive.

Dondar (dawn-DAHR): main city on Terlond's single continent.

Ebri (EH-bree): Yanda's birth father (Xentu).

Elznap: Shouma's planet; the powerful Sonda people.

ENAC: high end laptop computing device (Yanda has a 370; Seiti 420).

Eshet: blue moon of Terlond.

Farn: moon where Yanda was first imprisoned by Kridenit; no oxygen, only domes and night.

fems: females of humanoid species.

Flari: regeneration pool designed on Alland in the underground refuge, Pedore.

Frast: twisted Xentu, broke up the clan.

gallihoe: like a bus; powered by magnetic fields.

Gisli ("GIZ-lee"): from a small threatened planet; purplish-brown skin. Highly trained in military IT.

Great Stones: two moon-size stones within the planet of Terlond that are sentient.

Grethon: black smoke creature on Melcraf.

Hotel Dorador: in Sheffed; stayed in when shopped for Seiti's ENAC; off the beaten track, frequented by more unique clientele; funky, art deco façade.

Ilan: big red-haired man; can mind-read and shield powerfully; from Qontaq. Was part of the Alland underground when met Yanda.

jaja: a large, nearly extinct bird, only nests in sea caves within the elven forest. Petrified dung has powers.

japeet: elven term of endearment.

Jejod (juh-JOD): bird-like humanoids; warrior sisters: Aktat, Jat, Tik.

Jelat: one of the Keepers of Pedore; travels to Skarth often; tech whiz.

kaffe (KAF): coffee-like Terlondian drink.

Kridenit "Krid": evil mage; collects objects and creatures with powers.

lanten: form sea elves take, part sea creature.

Lark: Tenali's spaceship.

Melcraf: sister moon of Shalt and Ash-don, missing in Unknown Space.

Merne: a leader of the Neyna elves, Zamani's daughter, hair brown and green; can transform herself into any other being.

meshooli: fond Sonda term.

Mingal: a far planet at the edge of the known universe, all ocean.

Mnenu: male sea elf; leader of Ash-don's Circle.

mobri: one of Decru's power objects; obsidian like but shifts when exposed to certain elements.

Mons: Ilan's Qontaqi computer. Thin lead-gray, shiny, sleek. With powerful AI add-ons he melds with his own magic.

Nedri: Yanda's adoptive father from infancy.

Neyla: sea elves on planet Terlond.

Neyna: woodland elves of Terlond.

Omshi: Yanda's adoptive mother from infancy.

patat: Qontaqian marsupial.

Pedore: secret underground facility for those with powers, sequestered near the Church of the Vital Promise.

plaz: synthetic material made from recyclables or plant fibers; can be thin as paper or molded for furnitures, walls, roads.

plubber balls: large exercise balls.

Prokit's Moon (PRAH-kit): moon of Erzon, the Jejods' planet, Tlalit's favorite place. Artist and writers haven.

Qontaq: dynamic, sophisticated planet with conflict between those who have powers and those who don't.

Romden: Beri's planet.

Rotoul: elven forest on Terlond.

Salit: pale yellow-orange moon of Terlond.

Sandu (sahn-DOO): planet with large freighter business.

Sarsefi: Tlalit's spaceship's name, means lovemaking in Neyna.

Scaton (SKAY-tahn): startling cobalt blue and darker male elf, features hawklike, striking hob-nails boots. Can damper most powerful mind powers.

sedpods: single- or two-passenger bikes, some covered.

Senden Gares, or **SG**: secret branch of Qontaqi military that hunted powers for their own use.

Serstrop: passenger van.

Seiti: Yanda's daughter.

Shagal: moon where Seiti's image was caught on camera monitor.

Shalt: immense power stone of the Neyna.

Sheffed: rough borough of Dondar.

Shouma: woman with formidable mind powers, captive with Yanda.

Sinisay: a sinister branch of the Allandian government that monitors talent, prevents its use, sequesters its powers.

Skarth: main city on Alland, where Yanda was surgeon; large spaceport.

Sophis Tetra (SO-fis TEH-truh): powerful stone of the planet Goncha.

Sonda: Shouma's people; one of most powerful groups in the universe.

Soni: a Keeper of Pedore; healer, inventor of the healing tub, the Flari.

speradi: a most comforting fungus, used to make mushroom flour for baking.

squibbish: shrill-voiced bird of the Rotoulian forest.

Tadi ma grawn sa veyo: phrase from Tellotian people thought to have died out.

takla deets: sauteed mushrooms with delicate crisp filagree breading.

Telfer: Ilan's last name.

Tenali: half-elf grandson of Neyna leader, Zamani.

Tellot: gentle tropical planet where Gisli is from.

Terlond: planet of Yanda's captivity; where the elves live. Mostly ocean.

tesu: dolphin like, on Terlond.

Tik (teek): youngest Jejod sister.

Tiklet: secret school on Blaz for training children with special powers as weapons.

Tlalit: female wood elf; tangerine peaked hair; Merne's lover, ship captain.

Tregen: woman in Sinisay, sold out to highest bidders (Qontaqis, Blaz, Krid).

Tuk-tuk (TOOK-took): tiny primate native to Terlond with striking coloration, dark and gold.

Unknown Space: dark matter is different, hurts ship engines; little exploration there, no settlements.

Vashal: crystal pyramid in the Elven forest; houses the elven Circle trained to hold up the transparent protective dome.

Vatu: Yanda's close friend, fellow fugitive on Terlond; home planet Mingal, all water; can transform.

wagensi: "jerk", in Romden slang.

withum: flower whose pollen brings on a great mind-meld among the Elves one day a year.

Xentu: powerful, long-living people who have been missing from the known universe for some time.

Yanda: main character; was a surgeon on Alland.

Yandawi: Yanda's Xentu name.

Zamani: leader of the forest elves on Terlond.

Zami: Yanda and Zamani's son.

zad-flour: valued for its nutty flavor, used for baking in Mir establishments that cropped up in cities around the universe.

Zotoul: Neyla realm, including underwater city, and surrounding reefs and waters.

LIST OF ALL THE PLANETS
GROUPED IN STAR SYSTEMS

Star system: Berson Sector

Alland: (Yanda's home planet)

Shagal: (moon with wild trader city Blenin where Seiti was spotted)

Star system: Aband Sector

Terlond: Elves, captivity

Mir: [Farn is one of its four moons]

Star system: Craspel Sector

Romden: (Beri)

Tellot: planet of fragile, semi-tropical climate and nonviolent culture.

Dorn: planet known for high quality, innovative tech, often elegant in style.

Star system: Sentori Sector

Blaz: planet of traffickers, forced labor, mining and torture

Elznap (Shouma, of the Sonda culture)

Ontil (waterworld with unique sea creatures, many intelligent, such as Takmik)

Star system: Merdon Sector

Qontaq: (Bonden, Dele, Ilan)

Belsom: moon of Qontaq, city Lantat

Sandu: planet with large freighter system; Shouma's son and grandchildren

Erzon (planet of the Jejod; has Prokit's Moon)

Star system: Telori Sector

Mingal: sea world, Vatu's home

Marie Judson is an avid fantasy and sci-fi reader. She's been an editor, coffee roaster, and college professor. She lives on the wild coast of Northern California.

Visit her blog and sign up for her newsletter:

www.mariejudson.com

www.ingramcontent.com/pod-product-compliance
Lightning Source LLC
Chambersburg PA
CBHW050319110726
47899CB00007B/2298